# THE WAY I
# WAS TAUGHT

GLENN SCHIFFMAN

Published by **Roots & Wings Publishing**

*Western Gate Roots and Wings Foundation*

3131 Olympic Suite 304, Santa Monica, CA. 90404

www.wgrw.org

*Contact:* Glenn Schiffman Way(WasTaught@gmail.com

*Front Cover image:* Dallas Mathers – dallasdm@mindspring.com

*Representation:* Colibri Law Group - Culver City, CA 90232

# Acknowledgements

My profound gratitude extends to hundreds of people; not the least of which are my parents Merl and Mathilda Schiffman, my wife Barbara and my daughter Risa, my son-in-law Jared, and my brothers Joel, Hal, and Gordon. Writing teachers Kay Boyle, Stan Rice, Hal Grutzmacher and Bella Mahaya Carter and all the good writers at the Studio City Writers Group have influenced, taught and given me good notes and creative support; with thanks in particular to Dallas and James Mathers, and Leilani Squire.

American Indian teachers who have profoundly shaped my worldview include Wallace Black Elk, Twylah Nitsch, Marcellus Williams, Vincent La Duke, Albert White Hat, Jack Burnette, Fred Sitting Up, Eugene Black Bear, Mark Soldier Wolf, Robert Steed, and Richard Moves Camp.

To those 30-year veterans of Stone People Lodges, Native American Church ceremonies, vision fasts, and sun dances -- your loyalty, help and support have been critical. Miguel, David, Duncan, Walter, Ray, Tommy, Peter, Bob, Fred, Aziz, Billy, Bruce, Luis, Beau, James, Mike, Richard, Michael, Anthony, Virgil, Mark, Joseph, Mary, Laura, Martha-Lou, Sarah, Nancy, Shelley, Jenny, Amanda; the list goes on, but these Earth People in particular have been praying with me (in most cases) nearly half of my life.

GLENN SCHIFFMAN

"When some enormous power brushes me
with its clean wings,
I respond with Savage Intent.
I am an instrument of a hunt, an arrow shaft.
This book is my straying trail of blood."

(Annie Dillard, "Pilgrim at Tinker Creek")

# 1

## NATURE DOESN'T HEAR YOU WHEN YOU SCREAM

Halfway through my eleventh walk around the sun, I was charged by a bull.

Mother and I were at our summer cottage fifteen miles east of our hometown: Bethlehem, N.Y. Father was putting in his chaplain hours at the State Mental Hospital, an hour's drive west of us.

"Don't go in the DP's pasture," I had been told repeatedly by Birdie Mueller, the rich farmer's wife. "Don't trust that bull. Do you hear me, hon?" She called everyone 'hon.'

Even the tenant farmer in his pidgin English told me not to mess with the bull. The bull often had to be kept in a pen in the barn. The pen was across the hay drop from the stanchions that held the dairy cattle while they were milked, and was adjacent to the two stalls for the draw horses.

The horses were Belgians, a matching pair, black-brown in color; eighteen hands. One day, seeing me standing in awe of the draw horses, the tenant farmer's son, a fifteen-year old who spoke understandable English, said:

"The horses, okay. They like us." He motioned to the bull that was in the pen. "But that bull is..." He shook his head and made a chopping motion with his hand trying to find a word.

The son had numerous pock scars and black scabs on his right cheek caused by tiny worms that came off the flanks of cows he leaned his head against when he milked them. His pocked face usually distracted me, but what he didn't say about the bull… I heard.

The tenant farmer and his wife and son were "DPs," displaced persons, refugees from Eastern Europe. DPs were pre-judged by the locals to be on par with the reservation Indians. Every time school nurses found head lice, it was no longer just the Indian kids but also the DP kids who were suspect.

Head lice and a face full of wormholes made Mother shudder. Her city upbringing and college education kept the DPs at their proper distance.

Simon Mueller could afford electric fencing and metal posts, but the tenant farmer relied on old barbed wire and ash posts. When the tenant farmer felt his fence posts were put right, he let the bull and the draw horses out to graze. As long as there was good grass the cattle and horses were content to stay in their pastures. Come late summer with the smell of new mown hay and ripening corn – the fence lines were walked frequently to spot where the bull had rubbed against, leaned on, and weakened an ash post.

Our cottage was a former schoolhouse that my father bought in 1946. At the time of purchase it was a one-room building with a cloakroom, a potbelly stove, an outhouse, a well whose water was drawn by a hand-pump, and a woodshed. Over the next two years Father put in a stone fireplace, electricity, a sleeping loft, and an indoor toilet with a septic and leach-line. With those improvements, it became known as 'our cottage.'

It had no running water. Since we were rarely there in the winter, Father didn't bother to run plumbing "that would just freeze and burst." Water from the outdoor pump had to be hauled in a bucket to fill the toilet tank after every flush. It was my main chore, and it always took at least two buckets. I was nine years old before I could lift the weight of a bucket filled to the brim without sloshing it. Mother pumped the water she needed for cleaning and for cooking.

The cottage was on the east side of the south fork of the river, fifteen miles from Bethlehem by the Deer Hollow and Lost Hill roads and forty miles by the paved road.

No cars drove the dirt road from the west side down into the Hollow and back up again on the Lost Hill side. There were switchbacks down to the river on the west, similar hairpin turns marked the steep climb up the east side, and the roads on both sides were deeply rutted. Through the years enough cars had slid off an edge of the road or had been mired in the forest's run-off mud to convince people not to drive it.

Our one-acre lot was bordered south and west by an embankment and overlooked a gravel road four-way intersection called Drake's Corners. Old Man Drake lived in Old Fort and leased his farm, the bull, the draw horses and all the dairy cattle to the DPs. Drake would drive out occasionally to visit his farm and check on his tenants. Drake was a black-bumper Mennonite; his sect could own cars, but all the chrome had to be removed or painted black.

Simon Mueller detested Old Man Drake, so Simon lent my father the $100 to buy the lot and schoolhouse. That way Drake couldn't buy it. At least, that was the story I heard in passing… and that Drake was holier-than-thou. I heard those words bandied about.

Simon was president and patron of the 40-member Katakeskea, NY church where Father preached on Sunday nights. His 40-acre alfalfa field bordered the cottage lot to the east. North our lot was bordered by one of Simon's pastures. In that pasture was a giant elm tree that shaded the remnants of an old log house gutted by weather. The rotted floor was dangerous to walk on, plus there were probably rattlesnakes under what was left of the floorboards. Even so, I got wood from there to nail to the elm that helped me climb twelve feet to the first crotch.

I spent hours in that giant old elm. Afternoons I lay back in the three-branch crotch and watched the clouds, listened to the rasping crows, the noisy jays picking at acorns, the constant buzz of insects, far-off barking dogs, and sometimes the sound of a distant cowbell followed the bellowing of a bull.

There was a creek an eighth mile west of Drake's Corners. The road over the creek bridged a culvert large enough to allow the DP's cattle to pass from the north pasture to the south pasture under the road. The creek was deep enough to have minnows and frogs, pools of mosquito larvae, and all manner of water bugs.

I would stand on the culvert bridge and imagine I was on the Hornet, an aircraft carrier, in a B-25. I would run down the dirt road, arms outstretched like wings, and then take off, circle back and pretend I was part of the famous 1942 attack on Japan called Doolittle's Raid -- except my "bombs over Tokyo" rained showers of gravel on the minnows in the creek flowing under the culvert.

The creek fed a pond in the north pasture that had snapping turtles in it. The pond was half-covered with algae. Reeds and cattails grew around three sides and on the open side a willow, hundreds of years old, brushed the earth with her long silver-green leaves.

The pond always had an old-cheese smell to it, rendered even more rotten after a heavy summer rain when the stagnant, pungent water overflowed the low banks and brought tiny toads out from underground, upon which the raptors, the snappers, and snakes would feast.

I was told there were fish, bottom feeders, in the pond. I never waded in it. Quicksand was common in that area. I never messed with the snapping turtles. The big ones could cut a toad in half or take off a little finger with one bite.

When I knew the bull was in the barn or maybe in the south pasture, I followed an overflow gully from the pond into the old growth forest to the point where the thicket became impenetrable. I did look for openings. One time I brought a hand sickle, another time a hatchet hoping to chop my way in. I promised myself that one day, when I was bigger, I would follow the creek into the forest's witch darkness to where it emptied into the river. That dark forest lured me. I was Hansel; I was captivated by it.

One time standing at the dense gateway to that enchanting forest I heard a voice, a woman's voice, singing my name. That was the first time I heard her.

When I came out of the forest after hours of meandering, I always veered hard right and followed the fence line on the safe side, not knowing at that point if maybe the bull was in the north pasture. I crossed a weed field to get back to the road well west of the culvert. Most of the weeds were as tall as I was; some were as tall as September corn.

I trampled down enough paths in the weeds that I turned the winter game of 'fox and geese' into a summer game of 'lions and antelopes.' I was the lion, springing out of a hideaway in the weeds on some poor, scrambling non-existent antelope. The downside of this game were all the chiggers, mosquitoes, mites, flies, spiders, hayseeds, thistles and pulverized dirt that covered me from head to toe after I brought down an antelope. Thank God I had no allergies. Thank God my hair was buzz-cut.

There was no shower or bath at the cottage. I needed to get back before the sun went down so I could pour sun-warmed water from gallon bottles over myself, and soap down while standing naked in the mud around the hand-pump. Then I pumped a bucket or two of well water and dumped it on my head to rinse the soap. That well water was a constant 57 degrees, and it always made me shudder. It took all my resolve to pour out the first bucket over my head.

That summer of my tenth walk around the sun, I had a pet goat, a nanny that was often tethered to the pump. The nanny was supposedly pregnant. Since Mother was pregnant, Father reasoned that I would learn about birth from watching the nanny birth her kids.

The goat was very curious about me when I was naked. She nuzzled me and fluttered her ears and then backed into me. I threw cold water on her to make her stop. One time Mother saw the goat backing into me as I washed. Mother screeched like a barn owl:

"Stop that! What's wrong with you!"

Mother came over and yanked the goat's collar hard, making it choke. Then she grabbed the towel from the clothesline and threw it at me.

"Don't ever do that again!"

"Do what?" I wondered.

"Never mind."

"Do what??"

In the northwest corner of the cottage lot on a slope was a big oak. Father hung a long rope from a high branch and knotted the bottom with a knot big enough to sit on. I swung thirty-foot arcs out over the slope.

One muggy August day in 1949, my mother's birthday, we had a picnic. People from the two country churches my father served came to the remodeled country cottage.

Kids of all ages and some of the adults climbed on Simon Mueller's hay wagon and headed for the river. My mother and father stayed at the cottage with some of the older men and women. My father couldn't swim but was too embarrassed to admit that, and Mother never, I noticed, appeared in public in a bathing suit if my father was not close by.

Simon Mueller's brand-new John Deere tractor pulled us down to the shallows of the Deer Hollow ford below the dead end of Lost Hill Road.

My swimming suit was a hideous brown wool rummage sale item with yellow shoulder straps. The wool was scratchy when dry and smelled weird wet. I hated that swimsuit, but that day I splashed and cooled off and laughed at myself in my stupid suit.

Just before we left to go back to the cottage for hot dogs, macaroni salad, baked beans, coleslaw, Devil's Food cake, cherry pie, and homemade peach ice cream -- I heard for the second time a woman's voice singing my name.

I asked Suzy Vogel if she heard it. She was five years older and had to wear a bathing suit with a top. I thought she was real pretty.

She laughed: "It's the river, maybe there's an echo of our voices off the cliffs."

I shook my head. "It's not an echo."

"Or maybe you hear the Indian kids who swim down there. They say there is a waterfall and a pool somewhere down there. Don't go there. They will beat you up."

"I get along good with the Indian kids I know," I said.

"Anyway, it's a long hike," she continued, discouraging me.

*If it's so far, how could I hear them,* I thought.

A late day breeze licked my neck and tossed my cowlick. The thick forest smelled so good there. The cliffs that channeled the river reflected the gold of the August sun. I said nothing more and just stood, looked down river and heard a woman's voice singing my name, the same voice that I had heard at the edge of the forest.

On some perceptive level I understood another reason why Mother and I were parked at the cottage all summer the year of my tenth walk around the sun. Father had changed after he took psychology courses at the University of Rochester and got the job at the Bethlehem State Hospital. What I noticed was he enjoyed his time away from us, and he stopped talking so much at the dinner table.

Mother and I listened to the radio almost every night. "The Thin Man," "The Lone Ranger," "Fibber McGee and Molly" were on Mutual. "Jack Benny" and "It Pays To Be Ignorant" were on CBS. "It Pays To Be Ignorant" irritated Mother. She said the program "rewarded mediocrity." Fortunately for her, the old stand-up Motorola could pick up classical music on CBC from Hamilton, Canada. I turned on Buffalo Bison baseball games on WBEN, but not if one of her programs was on.

We didn't have a dictionary at the cottage. I had to wait until we got home to look up 'mediocrity.'

One night we heard some radio drama about a man who met a former girlfriend on a business trip and confessed to his wife that he had kissed her and he was all confused and trying to be honest and "never meant to hurt you." At the end of that program Mother was crying.

"What's wrong?" I asked.

"Never mind," she said and turned away.

One afternoon toward the end of August 1950, on the dirt road to Old Fort, I was batting stones with a maple branch I had whittled into a makeshift bat. The stones came from a rock pile the road grader had tipped into a hollow in the embankment. I had my back to Mueller's alfalfa field and was parking home runs across the road into von Koss' west pasture. I did not know that the DP's bull had gotten loose. The smell of Simon Mueller's fresh cut alfalfa was too much to resist.

The DP and his son found the bull and had pulled and driven it down out of the alfalfa field onto the dirt road. I turned to see them when they were just ten feet away.

The DP pulled a rope tied to the brute's nose ring and the DP's son was off and on swatting the bull from behind with a willow switch.

There was an angle cut footpath up the ten-foot embankment near where I imitated Ted Williams. When I saw that bull being pulled by the rope, its head stretched out long, its mouth half-open and dripping saliva and cud, its eyes bloodshot with anger, I turned and ran up the angle-cut path of the embankment.

At the top I stopped to look back, like some fool hero, assuming the creature would keep to the road. I did not envision it bolting, slamming forward, staggering the DP aside, yanking the rope free and leaving the son open-mouthed and startled in dust.

I froze long enough to imprint the sight of 800 pounds of snorting head, hooves, and swinging balls coming up the angle-cut footpath of the embankment. Even head-on I could see -- and have not forgotten -- the sight of that swinging nut sack.

I screamed and ran toward the cottage. I looked back once to see a curly-haired white head with rope dragging from a nose ring trotting fifteen feet behind me, while the DP and his son clambered up the embankment.

There were several obstacles affecting the bull's passage through our lot. The most obvious was the cottage, the door toward which I was running, screaming. The second was the goat, tethered on a lead to the hand pump. She was rearing and bleating and then dipping her head and defending. Right of the goat was the woodshed and then the old flagpole and its circular rock wall.

Fourth, left of the cottage was my pregnant mother, lying in a hammock. The hammock was strung from an apple tree to an eyehook ratcheted to the south cottage wall.

The bull chose the fourth route.

Half asleep and six-months pregnant, Mother did not move quickly. From the corner of my eye as I jumped to the door, I saw her fall from the hammock and crouch on the ground, cowering with white fear at the massive animal that was nearly upon her.

I clawed my way into the cottage and hid under the only table, frantically clutching my crotch to keep from pissing my pants. I heard ghastly wailing above my own fear-choked gasping and then… silence.

I crept from under the table. Through the front window I saw the back of the bull and the DP's son heading back onto the gravel road at the corners.

Through the screen door I heard the DP's voice, some Slavic muttering, and then another involuntary scream.

I skulked outside. Mother lay on the ground, blood dripping down the left side of her face. The ropes had been ripped and the hammock trampled and dragged ten feet.

The tenant farmer was standing over Mother. Both were inert, shocked, helpless. I looked away, unable to speak, not wanting to see.

The goat bleated incessantly but with a harsh sound. I saw that the tether had wrapped around her neck. I responded robotically and unwrapped the rope, un-choked the goat. I glanced at the road and saw the bull strolling up the road past the rope-swing oak. The tenant farmer's son walked beside it, holding the rope loosely. The son was twirling the switch in his hand.

"I go, I go!" said the DP, suddenly beside me. "Help," and then his suspenders and cord pants and sweat yellow shirt were running, goofy-like, toward his farm.

Father had yet to put in a telephone, "too expensive, and anyway it would be a party line" and of course the DP didn't have one. The nearest phone was at Simon Mueller's place, a half-mile uphill.

I sat on the ground next to my mother and tried to cradle her head. There was a puddle of water between her legs. I feared at first she was dead, but then a leg would twitch. Twice her belly seemed to seize. I watched my tears fall on her face. Her eye socket... the bone was crushed in... blood was coming from the socket.

I dug in my pocket for my clean white handkerchief.

"That's why we iron them," Mother once told me. "That makes them sterile. You can use them on wounds."

I wiped my tears and dabbed at the blood on her cheek. When I touched the cheekbone, she cried out with as mortal a sound as I have ever heard. But her eyes stayed closed, caked shut by blood.

"I'm sorry, I'm sorry," I whispered. Then to the sky I rasped, "Oh God, I'm so sorry!" But such convulsive sobbing clutched my words that they flinched, and then I felt warm forlorn urine trickling onto my left thigh.

After a few endless minutes the DP's wife came into the yard. I had never spoken to her but I knew her; she was unmistakable. She was shaped like a very large pear. She wore a grey muslin dress with a white apron and she had on a kind of hairnet white bonnet thing.

The wife spoke less English than her husband; but she took over, talking comfort to Mother in some Slavic tongue. One English word she did know was "baby." I understood enough of her sign language and pidgin English to look for clean water and clean cotton dish towels. While inside, away from judgment, I changed my pants.

Soon, the tenant farmer showed up with a homemade stretcher.

Then, Simon Mueller and Birdie and the DP's son arrived at high speed in their Cadillac, kicking up gravel, billowing dust. The DP's son, the one who spoke understandable English, had run the half-mile uphill to the Mueller's for help.

Birdie said they called the ambulance, but it could be a half-hour before it arrived. The nearest hospital was in Duck Lake, another twenty miles east, and most of the miles were gravel roads.

Even though the DP's wife seemed to know what she was doing, Birdie took over. The decision was made to put Mother in the Cadillac and drive towards Duck Lake.

They would intercept the ambulance somewhere on the only route between here and there. Having the stretcher on hand probably influenced that decision, though that was not likely the DP's intention when he brought it.

The DP's wife kept saying "No, No" and "House, Bed" but Birdie and Simon didn't listen.

I held the goat back from the path and Simon and the DP carried Mother on the stretcher to the Cadillac. Mother was placed across the back seat with fearful difficulty, and hearing her tortured moaning I turned away and hugged the goat with all my might.

Birdie put her hand on my shoulder.

"You shouldn't..." she started, and then, "Stay here, hon. We'll call your father. He'll send someone." She looked at the pear-shaped woman and hand-signaled and pointed at me.

As they drove off, the DP muttered, "Naw zee haw ya done."

I didn't know to or about whom the DP was talking.

The woman held out her meaty pink hand.

"Come," she insisted.

"No," I refused.

"You come!" she demanded and then pleaded, "Is good!"

"No," and that was that.

They walked off, speaking shlush and jzzz sounds and shaking their heads.

I picked up the hammock and tried to put it back together. I pumped a bucket of drinking water for the goat, but somehow tripped over it as I set it down, emptying it. I pumped another one. Then I sat with my back propped against the woodshed and sobbed hysterically, gulping and heaving with heart pain, stopping finally when the goat nuzzled me and I nuzzled her in return.

At some point the DP's son came by with bread that had some kind of paste on it. I refused it. There was food in the house; I would be okay. Anyway, someone was coming. Birdie said so. The son shrugged and left.

I tethered the goat in the high grass near the oak tree and then swung on the rope swing with guilt and fear as companions.

After a couple of hours Father Justus came along the Lost Hill Road from the west. He was in the St. Jerome's boarding school truck, a wartime model Jeep. The truck could handle the Deer Hollow Ford. Father Justus joked it could climb a telephone pole.

Father Justus ran the school and orphanage on the Zoar Valley Onodowaga Reservation. He was my father's cousin. They were descended from the same Irish family. Their mothers were sisters. The difference was that the one sister, my grandmother, had died in the flu epidemic in 1919. Then my paternal grandfather, an Evangelical German, yanked my father from the Irish family and set him on a Protestant path. Now one was a Catholic priest and the other a Protestant minister and, helped by the family rift, each 'Man of God' regarded the other with religious dislike.

"Get your toothbrush and some clean clothes. You'll be staying with us for a few days," Father Justus grunted, and then with a voice accomplished at disregard:

"The baby was delivered in the ambulance on the way to the hospital. It was a girl. Your mother is alive but unconscious. The baby died."

I dropped to my knees, clutched my gut, and vomited once, twice, and again. The dry heave acid burned my throat.

Father Justus muttered, "What possesses your father to leave a pregnant woman out here miles from help with only a coward for protection," and then from deeper in his hooded venom, "as if I didn't know."

The word 'coward' speared my heart.

"Get up," he hissed. "You're wasting my time."

I wiped my chin on my sleeve, caught my breath, and from my knees looked up at him. "How long we gonna be? I should water the goat, and put her on a longer rope."

Father Justus looked at me out of the shadow of Rasputin eyes. "It could be awhile; we can't take her. Just set her loose. She'll be alright."

"She'll get in the DP's garden."

"Well, then, they'll have meat for the winter, won't they?"

I looked at Father Justus' dark lashes and cur smile and thought: *at least she will be free – for awhile.*

# 2
# *WHAT COLOR IS YELLOW?*

The Catholic Diocese of the City of Buffalo built the St. Jerome Asylum for Orphan and Destitute Indian Children in 1900. It was administered as an orphanage until 1936. Backroom legal maneuvers in 1936 allowed the Depression-strapped diocese to sell the orphanage to the State of New York. It became the Jerome Indian School on the Zoar Valley Onodowaga Indian Reservation.

The diocese cleverly managed to maintain control of the administrative staff and some of the curriculum, but had none of the expenses. Their influence was so great that the locals continued to call the place "St." Jerome's.

The State of New York made several noticeable changes. A statue of St. Jerome was removed from the main lobby and a bust of Red Jacket was put on a dais in its place. Red Jacket, a brilliant orator who lived through the American Revolution and into the time of Andrew Jackson, was the most famous Onodowaga. He once said to a missionary:

"...You black robes say there is but one way to worship and serve Good Mind. If there is but one religion, why do you white people endlessly quarrel about it? We also have a religion, to be thankful for all the favors we receive, to love each other, and to be united. We do not wish to destroy your religion, or take it from you. Why do you insist on destroying ours?"

That observation was not etched in stone or scrolled on parchment and framed and hung on a wall. The bust was a bronze paean meant for mollifying. None of the true colonial history that subjugated the Onodowaga ever entered the Jerome classrooms.

The main building was a red brick three-story blockhouse with turret-looking structures at the corners. It had a wide, paneled front door, tall rectangular windows with decorative molding, window portals jutting from a sloping third-floor roof and a triangular structure on the roof in front that served no function other than to leak rain water into the third-floor dorm rooms.

After it became a state school, the bars on the first-floor windows and heavy steel screens on the second-floor windows were removed. As an orphanage it was basically a prison, and the Indian kids had to be kept from bolting for freedom; had to be prevented from jumping out of second-story windows. In the orphanage days even the doors to the fire escapes were locked. For fire safety reasons, if no other, these changes were critical and changed the entire emotional texture of the place. Movement was no longer restricted. During the school year, everyone but the true orphans went to their homes at night. In 1950 there were still a dozen plus orphans from the Zoar Valley, Oil Springs and Niagara Reservations living at "St." Jerome's.

There were dorm rooms on the third-floor, classrooms on the second-floor, and a cafeteria and offices and an "inter-denominational" chapel on the first-floor. There was a basement to which the residents were not allowed entrance.

Meals were served three times a day even to the non-resident students. There was a lot of oatmeal, a lot of spam, and a lot of canned soup. This practice encouraged school attendance, but it was also a form of welfare exploitation. The state was tapping the federal commodity food program that was a stipulation of a hundred-fifty-year-old treaty with the Onodowaga. Fortunately, bread was baked fresh in-house as flour and sugar were treaty rations and were to be supplied "as long as the grass was green."

After the state took nominal control, farm and vocational buildings were constructed behind the brick blockhouse. There was a quarter-acre vegetable garden and some flowerbeds. There were apple and peach and cherry trees that in 1950 were fully mature and full of fruit.

Boys were introduced to trades such as carpentry, auto mechanics, and the white man's ways of animal husbandry and agriculture. Girls were taught to type and run adding machines and switchboards. The girls also were taught to can fruit and vegetables and to cook in a large commercial kitchen. Some, not all, of the maintenance staffers, but none of the teachers or administrators, were former resident orphans.

The school covered grades 1 to 8. High school youths were picked up by bus every morning in front of the school and driven eight miles into Bethlehem, the reservation border town. It was not lost on the residents of Bethlehem that the Indian boys were superior athletes. The little town of Bethlehem made it to the Div. III state finals in track and in basketball almost annually because of the Indian athletes.

I spent the last week of August and the first three weeks of September 1950 at "St." Jerome's. I begged my father to let me come home, but he said I would have to stay at the Indian School until my mother was out of the hospital and settled.

"It's logistics," he said, as if I knew what he meant. "She is in a hospital fifty miles from here. By the time I get back it's late at night. They don't allow children to visit and I can't leave you alone in the house. It won't be for long."

Every morning before a breakfast of watery oatmeal, the permanent resident orphans and some local kids like myself who were temporary residents stood and faced a crucifixion hanging on a wall. One of the former "St." Jerome's administrators said something in Latin about all of us being sinners, and then the Catholic kids and others who didn't know any better crossed themselves. This was done even though it had been a state school fourteen years already.

A few of the older male orphans refused to communicate or cooperate and in other ways defied the teachers, administrators, and Father Justus. Those who were blatantly or persistently defiant ran the risk of a leather belt lashing. Whippings were less common once the state supposedly took over, but they did happen. Physical punishment only made those boys even more sullen and more insolent.

The best I could, I followed their lead. I refused to hand-curtsy the crucifix; I refused to speak, Latin or English. I hardly said a word to anyone for four weeks, and with one exception I did my clean-up chores to the least of my ability.

The chore I loved and did religiously and well was burning the trash in the incinerator out back of the kitchen. I loved burning things; I was fascinated by and loved fire. In Bethlehem, from the time I started school I would snatch matchbooks from the tobacco counter at Woolworth's and light the matches one by one just to watch them burn.

One older boy and I, a Cayuga kid named Lionel Halftown, collected the paper trash from all the offices, the schoolrooms, the kitchen; even the bathrooms – wherever there was a wastebasket. Lionel made me do the dirty work, dumping all the trash and garbage into a big metal trashcan that was on wheels. It took the two of us to roll it out and dump it into the iron incinerator.

For doing the dirty work, Lionel let me strike the matches and light the fire. I rarely spoke even to Lionel, not that he cared. I was determined to live the hours and days I spent at the Jerome Indian School in silence. I did realize that nobody, with the exception of Father Justus, cared if I talked or not. Nevertheless, I knew it aggravated Justus, so I kept it up.

Father Justus knew he could get away with whipping Indians, but the white boy who was also related to him by blood was treated to a different tactic: emotional torture.

Every day he deliberately called on me to answer a question or read from a catechism or lead the Lord's Prayer or pledge allegiance to the flag. Every day I mutely refused. Every day Father Justus made me then walk around with a sign hanging from my shoulders down my back that said "Dunce."

It infuriated Justus when I wouldn't say The Lord's Prayer.

"Do you want to burn in hell?" he fumed. "Do you want me to tell your father that you refuse to say The Lord's Prayer? Nephew! I'm speaking to you! Look at me when I speak to you!"

That was an empty threat. I knew my father wouldn't punish me for not doing Catholic ritual. There was no love lost between my father and Justus. Following his mother's death, the Irish side of Father's family was told by their priest to shun the German sinners and all of them did -- except my great-grandfather, David O'Sullivan, who owned a saloon in Crystal Springs on US 20 south of the reservation, and who apparently didn't like priests either.

Father Justus, not be outdone or outlasted by a mere boy, during catechism class on Monday of what turned out to be the last week I was at "St." Jerome's, changed the sign on my back to read, "What Color is Yellow?"

When I found out what it said, I spoke. I asked, "Why?"

In front of everybody, Justus smirked: "That bull didn't charge you. It was just taking a shortcut across the lot. Your cowardly panic caused the bull to tread on your mother and kill your baby sister. Your mother would be fine today except for you."

To call an Onodowaga boy a "coward," or to call someone "yellow" in front of a group of Onodowaga boys. was the worst curse imaginable, and Justus knew it.

White ice humiliation waved over me. I turned away, but there was nowhere to go but back to my seat. I dropped into it, bowed my head, and bit my lip until I tasted blood. My only way out was to wear the humiliating sign in silence and without tears. If I could do that, at least the tribal kids would give me credit.

On Wednesdays my father led a Bible class for the Protestants in the Quaker Meeting Room across the street. The chapel on the first floor of the school was supposed to be inter-denominational, but the big crucifix over the altar had never been taken down. The excuse was it was the only Catholic sanctuary and rectory for the reservation. My father refused to hold service under a crucifix and instead chose to meet in the plain, white, no-altar Quaker Meeting Room.

Some nights in the boys' dorm room on the west side of the third-floor, the whimpering and crying and restlessness of the true orphans in residence was painful to hear.

I lay on my metal bunk bed with its creaking springs and miserably thin mattress and blocked out the crying by retreating into dreaming about wandering the forest to a silent secret hiding place.

One twelve-year-old boy, Jimmy John, a name I thought was funny until he punched me a bloody lip for laughing at it, several times cried out from his dreams:

"Ewasata! Ewasata!"

There was so much hurt in it. I could not block it out. I lay there wondering what could cause that. I knew not to ask Jimmy John. I knew not to embarrass him. Indian boys took great pride in their ability to endure pain.

Minnie One Knife worked in the kitchen at St. Jerome's. She was Protestant, but she got the job because the state wouldn't let the administrators give all the jobs to the Catholic Indians. I knew her; she always came to Wednesday night Bible Class. She was a direct descendant of Red Jacket, too.

I waited until a Wednesday night when we were all across the street where Justus couldn't hear me speaking and I asked her: "What does 'Ewasata' mean?"

A wingbeat of alarm crossed her face, but then she softened.

"Where did you hear that?"

"Jimmy John – when he's asleep. He thrashes in his bed and moans and cries and sometimes he talks in his sleep and says 'Ewasata.' And he cries so hard, it hurts me to hear him, and I know Indian boys don't cry. Everyone knows that. Indian boys don't cry even in pain, but Jimmy John cries when he's sleeping. Other kids do too, but with Jimmy it is painful to hear."

Gramma Minnie – even Justus called her Gramma, such was her lineage and status – gazed at me impassively, looking past me or through me, for a long moment. I dropped my head and looked down, uncomfortable for bothering her.

She put her hand under my chin, lifted my head and looked directly into my eyes.

"Jimmy's parents... did not die in a... good way..." She paused and considered her words. "They were buried in a common grave with vagrants and criminals. 'Ewasata' means 'bury them'... properly. He means 'Indian Way.' In our way we would bathe them and paint them and wrap them in birch bark and then place the bodies between the roots of an old tree – Elm for most people, Maple for the leaders and warriors. Jimmy John is talking to his ancestors in the dream world. He is asking them to help his parents' souls find an Elm Tree."

Minnie One Knife's eyes glistened. "I tell you this because I can see you are old beyond your years, and because I respect your father. He has never talked down to us and he has never tried to force us to change our ways. I know you can see and hear what's real, and so I won't talk down to you.

"I've noticed that when you are across the street, you don't speak, and that's your business. About Jimmy John, for sure don't say a word to anyone! okay? Especially not to Father Justus. He calls us sinners. He might put a sign on Jimmy's back. If he did that, that's our business."

I swallowed hard and nodded "yes" and dried my eyes with my sleeve.

Gramma Minnie drew me close and gave me a hug. It embarrassed me and I ducked out from under her arm. I was not used to being hugged. Mother and Father did not hug me, nor did I ever see them hug each other.

Two days later while Father Justus was in his quarters listening to the Yankees beat the Red Sox in a play-off on a ninth inning homerun by Tommy Heinrich -- I burned the paper trash in the wastebasket in Justus' study. I just didn't bother to take the trash to the incinerator. I lit the trash in the deep metal wastebasket with matches I found in Justus' humidor. Once the fire was blazing, I took off the cardboard sign that said, "What Color is Yellow?" and fed that to the fire.

I watched, captivated by the way the wallpaper curled and crinkled slowly and then turned brown and then black. Even though I was only nine and three-quarters years old, I felt more than just delight at watching the word 'yellow' burn; I felt a deep satisfaction. It was the first time in my life I felt that. I understood too that the feeling came from a defiance of authority. The impact of that action and feeling would hold in me for years to come.

Minnie One Knife smelled the smoke and came running, towel over her shoulder, carrying water in a pot from the kitchen. She poured the water on the fire in the wastebasket, and smothered the small flames on the wall with the towel.

I thought: *That was interesting. I would have thrown the water on the wall.*

Gramma Minnie looked at me with kindred interest, and then said, as if in answer to my thought: "Always put out the Mother Fire first."

That was my first inkling that this sweet, earthy woman whom everyone called Gramma somehow could 'hear' thoughts.

Even setting the wallpaper on fire didn't get me kicked out of St. Jerome's as I had intended. Perhaps Gramma Minnie somehow covered for me, or perhaps it was because the very next day my mother came home from the hospital and on Sunday night I left the Indian School and the metal bed and the federal grey uniforms for good.

Nothing my father said prepared me for the injury to my once beautiful mother's face and mind.

She was in a wingback chair in their darkened bedroom. The only odor I could name was camphor, though there was other medicine smells I recognized and a stagnant odor that reminded me of a rotting log on a hot day. I feared that smell, because I thought death was in the room.

She turned to see me with her right eye because she was now blind in her left eye.

"Ah!" she choked, "What are you...? I thought you weren't coming home until next week."

Her left cheekbone was covered with a hard plastic plate, which gave her voice a sound like she was talking through a funnel.

Even in shadows the sight of her made me gasp, my distress audible.

"Oh Mother... I'm..."

She turned away, waving me off with a flick of her wrist.

I went to my room and choked on my tears, once again mired in misery.

The first two weeks she was home she was ruled, it seemed, by obsessive behavior. In the mornings she would vacuum and dust the living room and her bedroom and wash the inside windows in each. She would do this every day. Those two rooms were spotless.

After she was done dusting and washing windows and vacuuming, she would sit every afternoon on the piano bench in the living room reading a book Father would bring from the library. Most of those were poetry books.

She would put the books where she put sheet music when she played the piano. She would stare at the book with her one good eye. Occasionally she would turn a page. After she turned a page, her hands hovered over the keys as though she meant to begin playing. Then at some point her hands would drop to her lap and fold passively.

One day in the second week of her being home I came home from school to find her on her hands and knees on the 9-by-12 blue rug in the living room brushing with a horsehair brush the nap of the rug. It seemed she wanted the nap to all go in the same direction. She leaned very close with her good eye and studied the nap closely, brushing one way almost lovingly, tenderly, like she was brushing a baby's head. This act seemed to give her pleasure. She hummed a hymn as she brushed.

When she realized I was watching from the doorway (I was afraid to go into the room), she crooned in her funnel voice: "They say I'm not responding to the medicines." She pointed at the rug. "See, I am responding."

She looked up at me. "I see the tears in your eyes. I cry inside." She raised her hand to the left side of her face and touched her plastic mask. "My hair needs brushing. Is that why they cut it all off? The windows are scratched too, but I can't brush those out."

I stood there in stunned silence realizing my mother was 'off her rocker,' and assuming it was my fault.

On Sunday, two weeks after she came home, she took all her pain medicine and all her sleeping pills at once. Then she came downstairs, told Father what she had done, and collapsed on the floor. Father called the ambulance.

*She wants to die,* I thought as I watched them put her in the ambulance. *This is my fault.*

The hospital in Bethlehem, like the one in Duck Lake, did not allow young children visiting privileges, so I spent that night in the backseat of the '48 Chevy under a brown army blanket. It was an 'Indian Summer' moonlight night, but there was no peace in it. I watched my father through a row of windows pace the floor in the hallway of the old red brick hospital.

The next day, after making a dozen phone calls, my father took me back to St. Jerome's. "I don't want him coming home from school and finding her dead," I overheard him say to Father Justus.

I sat in the hall outside Justus' study and listened to the two men of God grimace, sneer, bicker and bite.

"It's just for a few days. I'm having Marina admitted to the State Hospital. She can't hurt herself there. When that works out, then Hunter can come home again."

"So what about your parishioners? Is there no one in your church who can put him up? Or do Protestants not practice Christian charity?" There was a Dewey smirk in Justus' voice.

"He has a history of running away. And he plays with fire, and people know that. That's why I can't keep him at home."

I thought: *I'm not a runaway. I'm an explorer.*

"Why doesn't your brother take him for a while?" Justus snarled.

"Joe moved to South Carolina, and he's an alcoholic, just like..." My father stammered to a stop.

"Just like? Just like my family, is that what you were going to say? Pot calling the kettle black – you and all your affairs..."

"You snake!" my father hissed back. It was a tail-rattling, bile-releasing, vitriolic standoff. "This is not about Hunter." I could feel Father rise up and take a stance. "It's about me. Why don't you admit it? The day my father took my brothers and me out of St. Patrick's, your family rejected us. I don't care, but why do you need to take out your pathetic hatred out on the boy?"

Father Justus didn't budge. "'Shew me the nine year old, I'll shew ye the mon!'" he said with affected brogue. Justus had never even been to Ireland, never been out of Western New York, but every so often he would fall into his version of Irish brogue. Maybe he thought it would give him validity. He was a short, floppy potato sack of a man; brown curly hair, dark fish-mallet eyes, and his growled smile lifted his upper lip like a dog defending his food.

I kept looking at the floor. Hanging my head with shame was becoming a habit.

"He's lazy, he's insolent, and he's dumb." Justus snorted. "He tried to set fire to my office! No, he can't stay here -- not another day. He's nothing but trouble. Show me the nine year old... " Justus might have been wagging his forefinger at my father like he did when he harangued people from the pulpit. "Mark my words, he'll never amount to anything."

"If you're trying to quote Aristotle, you jerk, it's 'seven year old.' At least get it right!"

Suddenly Minnie One Knife -- Gramma Minnie -- rushed by me, slam-opened the door and stormed into the chapel; gutsy for someone five feet tall and maybe a hundred pounds.

"'Stop it, both of you! He's right outside the door! Heard every word! Goodness, you're family, yet you act as if you have no relatives! Is this the example you want to set? I'll take him home with me if this is the way you're going to act. Trust me, he'll be better off with me. I have nothing to prove. I'm not Hanyoah!'"

With that she stormed out of Justus' study, grabbed my hand, and took me into the kitchen for oatmeal cookies and fresh raw milk.

"Hanyoah," the old Onodowaga word for "white people," literally means "The air is wrinkled." The word also describes rotten eggs, rancid meat, sour milk; anything organic that is putrid. Gramma Minnie beat a hasty retreat because she had just called a priest and a minister "rotten eggs," which was rash and in very bad form for her culture. Lucky for her, they probably didn't know what it meant.

# 3

# THE CLAY
# OF MY CHILDHOOD

The liquor of hemlock bark and the manure of chickens and ducks fermented the clay and the air of my hometown, Bethlehem, NY. The stench was strongest on the railroad trestle that ricketed above the brown water of the Katakeskea River. The trestle was less than an eighth mile downriver from the glue factory and the tannery. The glue factory used flatcar loads of hooves, leg shanks and membranes in their processing. Hides were tanned with chicken manure and hemlock. Both factories dumped their residue into the river. All of it eventually ended up in Lake Erie.

The Katakeskea River split the town of Bethlehem in half and then bordered the Zoar Valley Indian Reservation on the reservation's south side before it drained into the lake.

Even when I was only seven years old, I was not afraid to cross the railroad trestle. I walked the trestle in the middle of the tracks. I stepped from creosote tie to creosote tie. Between the ties I saw the chemical froth in the murky water curling around the concrete abutments that held the upright girders, but I couldn't see the bottom of our river. The water was yellow and full of brown sludge and the froth was usually a milky grey. Some days the water was streaked pink, even purple, from blood and hide scrapings.

It was a long bridge to my childhood reckoning, but I always felt safe crossing it. I knew the inbound freight came early every morning and the outbound ran only once and late in the day and neither came on Saturdays and Sundays. There were no passenger trains on that line anymore.

In good weather after school, I skidded down the hard clay bank to the south side flats to watch with fascination men in Mickey Rooney hats and collarless shirts churn white flakes into fifty gallon metal barrels of glue. Other men with names on their shirts and pencils behind their ears who lived in the tree-lined part of town drove the machines that loaded the barrels of dry glue into box cars bound for plywood mills, book binding plants, shoe soles, and "other useful household items."

From near the loading docks of the tannery I watched a crane lift huge crates of burlap-covered hides of horses, mules, hogs, and cattle from flatcars freighted from the General Mills slaughterhouse in Buffalo where (I heard said) neck bones, entrails, pulped spines and belly meat were canned as dog food.

I marveled at the stacks -- "ricks" they call them -- of hemlock. The tarp-covered mounds of chicken manure crumpled my nose.

On weekends I ventured past the factories to play kickball with the children of the soot-covered Serb refugees who worked in a foundry that smelted railroad track spikes and clamps, plowshares, mowing machine teeth, and other farm implement parts. The Serbs kept to their own enclave, an area east of the factories called Lodeville. On weekends the men sat on three-legged stools on worn stoops playing dice games and chain-smoking black-tar Turkish cigarettes into their charcoal-coated lungs while their kids played in the cinder street.

I never mentioned to Mother that I played "on the wrong side of the tracks" because I noticed how much she tensed when she encountered head-on any of the various factory workers – particularly the Poles who, free of Hitler and Stalin, had manipulated a way through the refugee camps in Austria to Port Townsend in Canada and then smuggled themselves, some said, into western New York State. For six dollars a day they mixed hemlock bark with chicken manure and chromium into a liqueur that tanned hides for Buster Brown's Shoes.

Mother kept a journal and wrote poems, all of which she kept in the piano bench along with her sheet music. I snuck looks at that journal, wondering what she had to say about me. About the Polish tannery workers she wrote: "The gloom of their devastating history is borne in their cave black eyes. They cannot hide their scars with orthodox beards."

The Brown Shoe Company owned the tannery. The Wynnham family owned Gowa Glue. In 1949 it was one of the premiere glue-producing factories in America. Ralph Wynnham was, they said, a millionaire, and he and his wife lived right there in Bethlehem in the big three-story Victorian at the corner of Main and Chestnut. They also owned the Savings and Loan that held the mortgages on half the real estate in town.

Gowa Glue hired generational locals and paid their labor in cash. A high-school dropout started at $.75 an hour, more than $5 a day! High school graduates started at $1.00 an hour!

I got no allowance. I had to beg Father for a nickel for a Musketeers candy bar. It was a once a month treat at best. I never had money to buy bubblegum or collect baseball cards like the Stafford kids who lived across the street. $5 a day was wealth to me, and when I imagined a million dollars I thought of Mrs. Buff-Orfington on the Jack Benny radio show we listened to on Sunday nights.

The Wynnham family ruled the town of Bethlehem. People talked about them in whispers. They drove a Packard and it is said that in the carriage house behind the main house there was a vintage car with a long hood and curtains on the back windows. At Halloween no kid my age or younger went to their door to get candy. No kid, that is, but me.

Even so, I didn't have the pluck to go to the front door. I went to the servant's entrance that faced Chestnut Street. Each time I surprised the cook. Each time she looked around the kitchen and then put a homemade cookie in my bag. Each time she asked my name. Each time she asked, "Who's your mother?" and when I answered she said, "Oh, her."

The freight train that carried the products of the town's labor crossed the trestle each workday around 5pm. Before gathering steam the engineer, a local named Garfield Holcomb who lived in an apartment above Pamela's Bakery, always blew the whistle as the train clicked on the tracks 100 yards behind our house.

Well, it was true, my mom was pretty, city-pretty.

Garfield Holcomb seemed to think so. "Prettiest woman in town, even when annoyed," my father used to say.

"Hunter was born at dawn in a blizzard," my mother wrote in her journal. "The ward nurse made me walk up and down, up and down, out to the window at the far end and back to my bed in the corridor, over and over, in an effort to push him out. But, willful from the start, Hunter took three days to be born."

There was a picture on her dresser of me at two years old with long blonde curls, a bow, and wearing a dress. Mother loved that picture; I hated it. I'm not a girl!

In the spring of 1943 my father snuck me to a barbershop. He did not tell my mother. I don't remember that first hair cut. I also don't remember, but do imagine, my father's stone silence and my mother quietly swallowing back her tears at the dinner table after my father burned (in the incinerator behind the garage) the entire girl's wardrobe in which Mother had dressed me for the first two years of my life. There are plenty of Father's stone silences and Mother's swallowed tears that I do remember.

Father burned the clothes but not the picture. It remained the focus on her dresser for years after.

In the late summer of my second year when I was but thirty months old, I'm told I wandered into a cornfield. No one found me; after five hours I emerged on my own.

*(Seven years later I asked Gramma Minnie why no one looked in the cornfield. It was right behind our house. "There's a spirit watching you, protecting you even today." Gramma Minnie said, "That time she kept the people away until she finished doctoring you. Her name is our word for the Northern Lights, but you call her Singing Woman and she says 'she likes that name, too.'")*

The voice I heard calling my name from downriver was a same spirit who had led me into that cornfield.

More than once in the two years following that incident, police had to search for me. At four years old I crossed Grove Street and slipped through the victory garden beside the Staffords' house. I found a way through the thick brush and rusted-out wire fence to tightrope walk the cement walls of the "Race," that part of the river that channeled a swift current into a narrow cut between high concrete walls. The racing water turned the turbines of the generators of the power company. It was a dangerous place and children were warned to stay away, but I wasn't afraid. The pounding pulse of the water thrilled me. I worked my way along the concrete wall to where I could see the water plunge into a tunnel mouth at the power plant.

Two other outcomes of that adventure lodged in my memory: the mouse-hair driver's seat of Louie Manzenetti's police car and the cringe on Mother's face when she opened the front door and saw him holding me by my collar.

Louie, one of the town's two daytime cops, had heavy dark brows and lazy thick lids that nonetheless failed to hide the contempt in his eyes.

"I found your little boy," growled Louie, "by the power plant... on the abutment above the race! Lady, you better keep an eye on this kid. If he had fallen in, there would've been no saving him."

My mother never answered back to men like Louie. Instead, she looked around to see if neighbors were watching. Police cars tend to draw out the neighbors.

Louie let me go and I trotted inside. Mother thanked him timidly and quickly closed the door. I trudged upstairs to my room. I knew Mother wouldn't punish me. I could count on her to wait and tell my father.

He would say sharp words that often made her cry, and then he would come upstairs and cuff me around a few times. Then he would tell me to go to bed without any supper. That was the routine.

In 1946 one of Mother's brothers in his army uniform passed through and stayed a night on his way home from post-war Germany. He spoke German fluently, as did my mother, and he told stories about guarding and interpreting the jail-cell talk of high command German officers in the year following the surrender.

At one point when he quoted a General in German, Mother looked around, and then in a low voice said, "Nobody in this town knows I speak German. This place is full of refugees. They make me nervous." Hearing that, I understood why she shrank from the Poles and the Serbs. Hearing that, I decided to keep my mouth shut about my heritage.

At the bottom of the staircase in the front hallway of our house was an antique spinning wheel. It was a big one with a wheel almost three feet in diameter. I spun the wheel every time I walked by. One day I saw an old woman sitting by it. It was odd; she pressed into the space between the wheel and the wall. In fact, she seemed to press into the wall.

She was a sweet old lady, and she resembled pictures of witches that I saw in the Grimm's book. That's how I described her during bedtime prayers one evening.

"God Bless Mother and Father and the witch at the spinning wheel."

"What did you say?" Mother whispered.

"There's a witch at the spinning wheel. She comes out of the wall and sits there. I've seen her."

"There's no such thing. Ghosts and witches are ignorant superstitions. You had a dream. Go to sleep."

"She's not a ghost," I protested. "She's not scary. She's got an apron and a bonnet…"

"I told you, there's no such thing. Stop this nonsense right now."

A week later Father took me to the state mental hospital five miles northwest of Bethlehem, where he was also a chaplain.

I sat in an office and answered some questions from a guy in a white coat. He had me play some baby games, putting round pegs in round holes, and moving triangles and squares around and fitting puzzle pieces.

"What do you want to be when you grow up?" he asked.

"An interpreter," I answered.

"An interpreter?"

"Yeah, like my uncle."

That night I heard my father tell Mother, "There's nothing wrong with him. Let him have some imagination, for God's sake."

"There's a difference between ignorance and imagination, George!" Mother answered.

Bonnie Presley was a round-faced chubby girl a few years older than me. She lived just down Grove Street in a house with a barn, chickens and a mean pig that rushed the slats of its pen whenever I came close. Even in good weather Bonnie and her mother didn't take the shortcut via the railroad trestle. They walked the long way around, crossed the Main Street Bridge, then turned left onto Riverfront Road in order to meet Bonnie's father and brother on Friday nights at the Depot Hotel.

The Depot Hotel was a bar with upstairs rooms. The glue factory workers congregated there every Friday. The foundry workers drank at the Serb Hall in Lodeville in a building built in the 1920's for the Masons. On Friday nights many of the Poles who worked the tannery went to some place called the Temple in a town ten miles closer to Buffalo. They must have done their drinking there.

In good weather Bonnie played on the red bricks and iron railings of the Depot porch and got a hot dog and a coke as a reward for her patience. The brother, Ronnie, just seventeen and a high-school drop-out, sat inside in a booth with his parents. They bought pitchers of beer. Ronnie drank his beer from the tin cup of his thermos. He smoked Lucky Strikes.

One Friday night after supper during early June in 1948, my father found me hanging out on the steps of the Depot with Bonnie Presley.

The next day and then again on Sunday afternoon my mother put a dog leash on me, the kind that goes around the shoulders and clips at the back so I couldn't unhook it, and then she tied me to the railing of our front porch.

Going missing for five hours in a cornfield didn't cause Mother to tie me to the porch; playing by the Race didn't cause it; even playing with kids from Lodeville didn't cause it. But the Depot was an appalling place to my mother.

"A house of ill repute" is what she wrote in her journal. "A bar with upstairs rooms" is what she said out loud.

Tied to the porch the second Sunday I heard a rustling sound and I saw a spirit in the bushes by the porch. He was about a foot tall.

Friend (I named him "Friend") taught me to jump up and click my heels three times before landing. That I could do that at the age of seven impressed my father. As he cut me loose from the leash, he said, "Where did you learn to do that?" I just shrugged. I had learned not to tattle on witches and spirits.

Mother had a teaching credential and was a substitute teacher for high school grades, all subjects, for the local school district. She was also on the board of Bethlehem's little thousand square-foot library. She taught me to read before I started school, probably about age three. I learned to read with no effort. I heard people say I was gifted. Maybe so, I skipped kindergarten and started first grade at age five. I do know that the times Mother was teaching me to read were the only extended periods we spent together once she stopped dressing me in girl's clothes.

At five I easily read the cartoons on the back page and the big letters on the front page of the newspaper. At seven I knew that Truman was President and Dewey was Governor. I knew that DiMaggio played for the Yankees and Ted Williams played for the Red Sox. I also knew that Jackie Robinson played for Brooklyn. There was a photo on the wall in my father's study of Father shaking hands with Eugene Robinson, a black preacher at the Riverside Church in New York City. For a while I thought my father knew Jackie Robinson.

There were a dozen or so books I read over and over; six *Bobbsey Twin* books, *Bambi, Lightfoot The Deer, Tom Sawyer, Huckleberry Finn, Toby Tyler,* and *Richard Halliburton's Complete Book of Marvels.* But the book that rocked my fantasy was *Simba, King of the Beasts* by Osa Johnson. *Simba* was about an African boy and an American boy on their own in the East Africa grasslands after their Arab guide died from a cobra bite.

In one of the early chapters a lion had been killing cattle. Three hunters, including Simba's father, were chosen to tether a calf as bait, and then kill the lion. Simba, the boy, snuck out in the middle of the night and followed the hunters. Of course, they heard him, but it was too late and too dangerous to send him back to the village. Simba witnessed his father and the two other men kill a charging lion with their long spear-tipped lances. I must have read that chapter five times. My name was Hunter. That chapter gave my name meaning. It gave my name courage.

# 4

# *NO IDEAS*
# *BUT THINGS*

School at Bethlehem Central began every year near the end of September because half the student body lived on farms and rode school buses. During the first three weeks of September the farmers' kids were needed to help bring in the second crop of hay, thresh the feed corn, and pick apples.

One three-story building housed kindergarten through high school. At the far south end was the kindergarten: a large sunlit room with an inside area for naps and a built-in sandbox. At the extreme north end of the building was the senior boys auto shop and metal working shop. In the middle were the administrative offices, the auditorium, the gymnasium, and the cafeteria.

I was a grade ahead, had been a grade ahead all along, having skipped the sandbox. I was reading at a high school grade level at nine years old and though I was the youngest in my fifth grade class, I was a decent enough athlete that I was never the one picked last.

My fifth grade teacher, Miss Elman, sure did ripple the town gossip mill. She was a new hire and she was the first Jewish teacher ever at that school. Me, I was happy to be assigned to her class. Miss Elman was real pretty, I mean

40

Veronica Lake pretty, but with dark hair and blue eyes. And to top that she had big breasts and wore dresses and blouses that showed them off. Everybody said Mr. Chafee, the bone-bald principal, hired her because she was young, gorgeous, and built like a brick "you-know-what" as Sandy DiMitri pointed out.

"What?" I asked just one time.

Sandy looked at me like I was a turd in a toilet.

"A brick shithouse, stupid," he laughed. Sandy's father owned a barbershop, one I couldn't go to because of the magazines. Sandy was a sixth grader, so I figured he knew what he was talking about. Since I did not associate shithouse with outhouse, I thought he was talking about a building at the tannery where they stored the chicken manure they used in the tanning process. But I never noticed a brick building there.

"Who cares if she's Jewish?" Horace Bailey, our church's head usher, said to Ray Eggles. "She sure makes my bird-dog point!"

Horace worked at the state hospital and had a yard full of chickens at his house. We bought eggs from him. I didn't realize he had a bird- dog. He must have kept it in back, away from the chickens.

One thing I did notice, every time Miss Elman leaned over to look at my work there were whiffs of glamorous perfume and flashes of flesh, and I got hot under the collar.

My mother spent six weeks in the mental hospital and then three more weeks in a hospital in Philadelphia where she had reconstructive surgery.

While she was in the State Mental Hospital, I went to visit every Saturday. She wasn't in lockdown or anything like that. She had a nice room on a first floor and it even had a patio with a high wall so she had privacy. At first it was uncomfortable, weird even. I almost wanted to tiptoe around her, but after the first two visits I think she was almost glad to see me. I would bring her books and showed her my collection of postmarks I cut from my father's mail. He got a lot of mail from all over.

The fourth week I brought an essay, the first one I ever wrote, for her approval. It was about Lincoln. Mother complimented me because I hadn't made any spelling mistakes, but she corrected my grammar throughout the three pages. She called one sentence a dangling participle. She wondered why my teacher didn't correct that. I wanted to shout, "It's fifth grade! I don't even know what a 'participle' is!" But I didn't.

Philadelphia, actually Bala CynWyd (I had a postmark and knew how it was spelled), was where my mother grew up, near where she got her teaching credential at Villanova, and where her parents lived. After the reconstructive surgery at the medical school at Villanova, she spent several more weeks in my grandparent's care. Her parents paid for her surgery, which is why she went there to have it done.

I didn't much know my grandparents on my mother's side. I knew my grandfather was a judge. I knew my grandmother had something called Parkinson's disease, and there was a live-in nurse and maid, which was therefore good for my mother, too. I hadn't met them. They never came to visit us in Bethlehem. Only Mother ever went to visit them. I think there were bad feelings between my father and the Judge.

When I asked my mother why they didn't visit, she said, "It's because of the Parkinson's. She can't travel." When I asked my father, he said, "Your grandfather did not even attend our wedding because he felt your mother was marrying beneath her 'station.' He could hardly be bothered to visit us."

They always did send me a Christmas present though, usually ten dollars, which was a lot of money and which my father took and put in a savings account.

"For college," he always said. Before I was even nine years old I was made aware I would go to college and was expected to sacrifice even gift money to pay for it.

My mother came home by train a few days before Christmas. Instead of going to Buffalo, Father drove all the way down to Jamestown to pick her up. He said he didn't want her to have to change trains more than once. I didn't understand, but so what. At least I got to go along.

The surgery almost repaired her face. Her left eye was still blind, there were blood vessels showing, and she wore a wig, but she didn't have to wear the plastic mask anymore,

At first she didn't recognize me. I must have grown some, or maybe because it was winter and my freckles were down. She looked startled when I said, "Hi, Mom." Maybe it was the word 'Mom.' I usually called her 'Mother.'

We rode the seventy miles home in almost total silence. I sat in the backseat and wondered why, but was afraid to ask.

The surgery did not help her overcome what Father confided was called "atypical depression." He was trying to help me understand.

"She will have a few good days among a lot of dark ones." I took it as a warning. It meant more tip-toeing around.

Christmas Day was not one of the good days.

Every year up to then, Mother put up elaborate Christmas decorations. The front porch got lights and suspended angels and a full-scale manger. She liked pristine snow so I was not allowed to roll a snowman or build a fort. Rolling up a snowman made the yard look like "the dog's breakfast," as she put it.

A week before Christmas, Father would cut down a tree from the forest near the cottage. White bed sheets were put up over the two doors to the living room, and I was not allowed in the living room until Christmas Eve. Mother would spend a week decorating the tree with antique ornaments and lights that looked like candles. She then carefully placed, one by one, the tin-foil icicles she had daintily saved from previous years. My father would put a Lionel train set around the tree. He had bought it for himself before the war and it was not considered a toy. It only came out of its original boxes at Christmas time.

This time Christmas was different. It wasn't 'her' Christmas. We had a tree, but with just the lights, no ornaments and icicles, and there was nothing on the porch. Oh yeah, Father did get the Lionel train out. For the first time, he let me help put the tracks together.

"Take it easy! Don't bend the prongs! This will be yours, someday."

On Christmas Day we sat on the sofa in the living room after eating a 'Danish' for breakfast. Father handed Mother a present. She unwrapped the used icicles from the year before.

"I know how much you like to put on the icicles," he said.

The look she gave him, I wanted to run from that look, but it was Christmas.

She got up, pulled a handful of icicles from the box and flung them at the top of the tree.

"There," she said, and sat down and began crying.

I wanted a pair of ice skates, but instead I got a board game called "Meet The Presidents." I got that crisp $10 from my grandparents and pretended to look for Hamilton's face in the President's game. I knew Hamilton wasn't a President, but I wanted to hide the money under the board game.

Father saw me tucking it away. "It's not enough that they rub my face in how rich they are; now you insult me by hiding this. What are you planning to do with this?"

"Buy ice skates," I started to say but was cut off by my mother.

"What is this?" She was looking at her present, William Carlos Williams' only published book.

"Williams graduated from Villanova," Father said. "I thought you would appreciate that."

"What were you thinking?" she said. "He's... clinically depressed!" Her voice trailed off as she looked at me.

"But these poems are uplifting. 'No ideas but things'," Father protested.

"Williams went to Penn, not Villanova." She set the book on the coffee table and didn't give it another look.

There were a few other little things, stocking gifts, but I don't remember them. Oh, my father got a bottle of olives and a bottle of wine from our church's secretary, the owner of Bethlehem's only liquor store, one of the places where I stole matches. She gave the same present, olives and wine, every year. Her name, Kohler, was the same as the name on the faucet in the bathroom.

Mother wept into a lace handkerchief off and on all Christmas Day. She 'declined' to make the traditional leg of lamb my father special-ordered from Vogel's Meat Market. My father tried. It was cooked and all but wasn't the same.

It was my job to mash the potatoes. We had this contraption where I squeezed two handles together and the potatoes squeezed through holes in a basket. His potatoes were so hard I lost control and dumped the bowl of potatoes and the contraption on the floor. My parents were in the dining room talking with low voices, so I scooped all the lumps up and put it all back in the bowl. I remember his gravy was lumpy, too. There was no mint jelly. We didn't use the good china.

The olives were good. Father drank all the wine.

The day after New Year's, 1951, my mother went back to Philadelphia. This time my father drove her all the way. I was told there was some legal problems to take care of, insurance and something about guardianship.

"It's because we were married there," my father said. I did not know and was not told that they were getting a divorce. He was gone two weeks. I did not see Mother again until the next October.

# 5

# *HURT THESE THINGS, WE HURT OURSELVES*

Those weeks of January 1950, while my father was gone, I stayed with the One Knife family on the rez. I slept overnight at Gramma Minnie's house, walked a half-mile to "St." Jerome's in the early morning cold and snow with Gramma and her grandsons, and then took the school bus into Bethlehem to Miss Elman. It was tiring, but I didn't mind. I loved Miss Elman, even in the wintertime when she wore wool sweaters and an ordinary perfume. I was so in love with her, I never missed a day of school throughout fifth grade.

Minnie One Knife was then only in her forties, but she had two grandsons, one my age and one two years younger, who lived with her and her father, Haksot Jake One Knife.

Mavis and Norma, the mothers of the grandsons, lived and worked in Buffalo, sent money and rarely came to visit. There were high school pictures of both girls around, but none past sophomore. I never met the boys' fathers. I knew one of them was in prison.

The boy my age was called Nick. Mavis was his mother. Norma's boy was named a real long word that meant "Little Dry Hand." He had a cleft palate, his nose was deformed, and he was "slow," that is, retarded. He once spoke single words and parroted phrases like "Let's go to school," but in the past year had stopped talking, though he still made grunting noises. Physically he could do six-year-old things like use the bathroom and dress by himself.

"One of God's children," Gramma said. "Pure innocent. Pure kindness. Never judges anyone."

His nose was constantly running due to its deformity, so by age three Little Dry Hand had been nicknamed "Oskee," which meant "runny nose." The nickname stuck, although it wasn't long before Hawk Clan boys taunted him by calling him "Snot." Nick was fiercely protective of Oskee and stood up to anyone who teased his little brother. He got into many fights with Hawk Clan boys.

Actually, for six-years-old Oskee was a big kid, almost my height. Nick was taller than me. Haksot was short and skinny. The boys' fathers must've been tall.

My father told me Oskee had fetal alcohol poisoning at birth, and though I didn't know what that meant, I didn't pursue an explanation. The word 'poison' was enough and it was said in a whisper.

Oskee spent five days a week at the Jerome Indian School where Minnie One Knife worked and could keep an eye on him. On Wednesday nights he and Nick would sleep over in the dorm so Gramma could go to Bible class and not have to get him back and forth in the dark. On any extremely harsh winter night Gramma, Nick, and Oskee would stay over. Jerome's was like their second residence.

Haksot (it meant 'great grandfather,' and was a respectful title for all male elders) was gruff and sometimes hurtful. He had 'bowl-cut' white hair, leaned on an ironwood walking stick, and winced and griped about "witches' spears" in his hands and legs.

"You staying with us? For how long? When you leaving?" were his first words to me.

"Haksot!" Gramma snapped.

"We got mid-winter ceremonies coming up. He can't be here for that."

"He's staying till his father gets back, two weeks, maybe more."

"What his name?" he said to Gramma.

"Hunter," I said.

"See? He talks direct to me. No respect."

"Haksot, that's old ways. Let it go."

"Old ways is good, at least right now. Got ceremonies comin'."

He finally looked at me. "Hunter, huh? Powerful name. Have you earned that name?"

"I dunno."

"Haksot!" Gramma Minnie warned. "Give him peace."

"He said he don't know!" He looked back at me, "A name like that and you don't know... I heard you're a runaway. We don't have a word for that. Our children don't run away from us, they only run from your people." He looked back to Minnie. "So what do we call him? Kwayo? Rabbit?"

"My friends at school call me Hunt. I like that."

"You do, huh? Come summer, we'll go hunting, then we'll see. Until then, I'll call you Kwayo."

Gramma Minnie and Haksot were 'Earth People,' and taught their grandchildren traditional ways, language and logic, which included instruction about witchcraft, evil spirits, and a matter-of-fact relationship with death and dying. Whenever I was there I was included in the teachings.

We sat at night in the kitchen, the warmest room in the house. Gramma would sew by the light of one bare light bulb while Haksot told stories, "Good stories, not those 'why the rabbit has long ears' or 'why the dog licks his balls' stories the Clay People made up to make us look stupid."

Gramma sighed. "Everything is from one blood, stones, water, sky, even Clay People. Haksot, the old ways don't include despising people! This boy is a prayer of the Earth. I can see that in him."

Haksot rolled his eyes and grinned.

"Long ago," she said, "The four-legged and the wings and the five-fingers all talked with each other... Creating made it that way. Respect all life because we are related. We are all one blood. Hurt others," she said, "we hurt ourselves."

"He's a Christian! One blood means what Creator put on our land. Those people come from across the ocean. That's not one blood the way I reckon it!"

Gramma would give up for a night, but be back two days later with her universal message.

"Sacred things go in a circle. The breath of life, Elder Brother Sun, Grandmother Moon, Mother Earth, all are round. In that roundness," she said talking with her hands even while holding pins and needles "is knowledge and wisdom. Knowledge is a woman. Wisdom is a man. In the center of that roundness is a Fire, the first image created. Fire is both a man and a woman. Heat is the woman. Light is the man."

Haksot butted in often with statements like: "What the Clay People, you Christians, did was leave the woman out of it. The way, the truth, the light, but no woman, no heat. Three's not a sacred number. I'll take a four-legged stool any day."

Gramma wouldn't give up or give in.

"Long ago," she said, "Earth people used power with knowledge and wisdom; but when we began living in square houses and thinking in straight lines, we moved off the Earth and into the world; we forgot knowledge, we lost wisdom, we misused power."

Nick and I would sit at the table and listen. From time to time Nick would grunt, "Ungh!"

That grunt was so characteristic of the Onodowaga. It was a sign you were listening, even if you weren't. It took me awhile to pick it up.

Gramma Minnie, like many others in the Wolf Clan, was a Protestant because Protestant was less hassle than Catholic.

"They're so busy," she would say. "Up and down, my knees can't take it. Same with the hand flecking. And what's with the gibberish? They tell us not to speak our language, and then they groan on and on about dominoes." She smiled at her old joke.

Haksot had no truck with any churches or any Christian ceremonies or holidays. He called all priests and ministers "black-coats," only he usually put the word "goddamn" in front. He called all Christians 'Clay People.'

When I asked, "Why?" Gramma said, "The Bible. It says your God made you out of clay from a desert. Our people, we were made from rich forest earth. Humus; it's the root of human."

"Goddamn black-coats," Haksot bellyached. "Look at the effect their preaching has on the Clay People. Has it done any good? Has it made anyone more honest? Until it does, I will never follow a black-coat."

"The boy's father is a black-coat," Gramma said softly.

"Nah," I said. "Father Justus is a black-coat. My father is more like a grey-coat."

Haksot looked at me and laughed. "I'll say this for you, kid. You got 'onojah'."

"What's that?" I looked at Nick.

"Teeth. It means you bite back," Nick said.

"It means lots of things. It means we like you," laughed Gramma. "It means you have a sense of humor."

The One Knife family home was a two-story frame farmhouse, miserable for paint, two miles by road and a half-mile by bird's flight from the Indian School. Gramma and the boys walked that half-mile every day, on snowshoes when necessary. Through the years they beat a path across her twenty-acre peach grove, then through a big lot of Christmas trees leased by a doctor "as a tax dodge," Gramma said, to a cut made in a thicket of cottonwoods and willow, and then across a double-log bridge over Little Ghost Creek.

That was the beaten path we took early every morning those weeks while my father and mother were in Philadelphia. It was cold; the snow on the path had such a hard crust, we didn't need the snowshoes.

The bridge across the creek was covered with ice-packed snow and was real slick. We always helped Oskee across. Gramma would guide him and Nick would hold him from behind. I trailed. Oskee would whimper with worry, but he always made it. After the creek we trudged through the back-forty of a cornfield and a pumpkin patch before we arrived at the barns and craft buildings of "St." Jerome's.

East, a football-field distance from the log bridge, was a thicket of what had been a planted hedgerow a hundred years previous. It was overgrown with Hackberry,

Sweetgum, Bush Honeysuckle, Button-Brush, Slippery Elm and Tulip Trees.

I had been able to see that dense thicket from the third-floor of Jerome's when I was there in the fall, and I always felt a dark menace about the place. I knew the Tulip Trees had winged seeds big as robin feathers, and it would have been fun to drop them from the third-floor windows to see them helicopter in the wind. But the scary feeling stopped me from going there and collecting them. In October when the hedgerow stunned the eye with yellow, orange, scarlet, and even purple foliage, and crushing fallen licorice-aroma Sweetgum leaves under my feet was a favorite pastime, my dread still kept me away.

One cold early morning on the way to Jerome Indian School and the school bus to town, I noticed a Blacktail Deer, a doe, over by the hedgerow. She was looking right at me. There was something about her. I stopped and stared back, enchanted.

The doe flickered her tail and turned away, then turned back. I felt she was calling me, beckoning me. Even a hundred yards away, I felt I could see into her brown eyes.

"What are you looking at?" Gramma said, suddenly standing beside me, still holding Oskee's hand.

"There's a doe... it's like she talked to me."

"You can see her?" Gramma looked at me with amazement. "Really."

"Yeah, well, she's gone now..." I blinked. Where did she go?

"That hedgerow is a guardian. Those bindweeds are no accident. It's protecting some kind of dark power. She beckoned you, didn't she?" Gramma motioned toward where the deer had been.

I nodded 'yes.'

"What's behind the hedge, it's not from Good Mind. Tell him," she said to Nick.

"Blacktail Deer are a Dark Spirit lure. Don't ever follow them when they beckon," Nick said matter-of-fact.

"Don't go there, you hear me?" Gramma got real stern and looked hard at me. "It's Hungry's place. Fat Face could take you away if you go there!"

A shiver bolted through me at that. "Fat Face" was always mentioned when the talk was about the dead and dying.

But that very night I dreamt I was in the thicket, the old hedgerow. It wasn't winter, it was an Indian summer day in deep autumn. I was crunching Sweetgum leaves and the perfume of them was like the perfume Miss Elman wore.

There was no sound. The fragrant floor mat mulched silently beneath my feet, and the rushing water in Little Ghost Creek was mute. Witching insects flicked about but made no hum or buzz. No birds sang. Then the honeysuckle vines closed silently into a wall behind me.

I knew I was dreaming, but it was so real, especially when a cold wave shadowed through me, planting fear in my stomach and ragging dread on my palms. All of a sudden, I was on my knees, limp and weak with fright, my throat choked shut.

Something or someone with ethereal texture, which or who, with a paddle -- it felt like a paddle, or a turtle shell rattle -- struck me hard four times across my shoulder blades.

I pitched forward flat out and into quicksand.

Hands and forearms were swallowed by the muck, but my chin felt a crusty edge.

I curled my spine upwards, head back, chin high, and slowly wormed my arms side to side to create an air pocket in the quicksand, as if I knew to do that; to bend back, my eyes straining to see those air pockets while my feet grabbed a toehold on a tree root. The instant there was an air pocket I would yank my arms out…

…and wham, something or someone paddle-slammed my shoulders again. This time I knew it was the flat side of a turtle rattle. I heard the rattle sound.

My chin hit wet mud. I yanked my head up, and the muck beneath it pooled water, then gulped the water down. My arms were in it up to my shoulders. It was too wet, there was never going to be an air pocket, I was being sucked in head-first.

The wallow milked at my arms like a suckerfish gulping air. My chest just touched the cracking crust on the edge. A sheering slivering cry of panic at last escaped my throat.

"Help! HELP ME! GRANDMOTHER!!"

I heard a sound, a voice, ask, "Now?"

I turned my head to the right towards the south, my left ear an inch from the wet silt. In the bark of a Slippery Elm was the fat face of an Old Woman, hunched in the flow of the trunk, a mask of the tree, observing me with hawk nose, snipe ears and owl eyes.

"Now!" She called, low and soft. "Do you want to die now?"

Was she giving me a choice?

"Now?" Again, low and soft.

"No!" I said. "Not now."

My whole body seized. I kick-bounced upwards, left the ground, twisting right and then left. There was a popping sound of air pockets in the quag. Someone, something pulled my feet.

I was suddenly inside my shirt. My head was inside my collar, my arms inside the long sleeves of my flannel shirt. I wriggled backwards, hips and ribs snaking, the quicksand grabbing my shirt. Released, I got to my feet. The shirt spread-eagle sank into the hungry muck.

Air belched from a catch below the surface. A blow-by of wind hit me full force in the chest. I staggered backwards; tripped on a root, fell...

...and woke up in a death fearing sweat on the cold floor of Nick's bedroom. My back stung as though it had been slapped. I was exhausted.

"You all right?" Nick asked.

"Ah! I... I had a nightmare."

"You woke me up. You were sayin' 'help me, help me'."

"Yeah, yeah, sorry, it was scary. It was so real. I thought I was gonna die."

"Good thing you woke up, huh? So now, go back to sleep. We got things to do tomorrow, get ready for midwinter dance."

The following Saturday when Nick, Oskee and I came in from the barn after feeding the horses and other livestock, Gramma Minnie was standing at the sideboard, singing softly, kneading dried chokecherries into raw back straps from a deer.

"Can I help?" I asked, curious.

"You don't know the song."

I walked away wondering, "What is that all about?" so she said:

"The song prays that 'we all live to see the green grass again.' It's for the midwinter festival at the Long House. Haksot offers this pemmican during the Thanksgiving Prayer. Once it was an eight-day ceremony, but now only the main dance and the Thanksgiving Prayer are done at the Long House. Dream-guessing we do here. The peach stone gambling game and the white dog sacrifice are outlawed."

"Can I go?" I asked, hoping.

"No, you have to be Onodowaga. You will likely be here, though, when the False Faces bring new coals from the Long House and drive the winter spirits and all the illness out of the house."

"That's good. I like that part," said Nick. "These men, they wear these masks they cut from trees. They crawl in on all fours, and if we don't get on all fours too, they slap our backs with turtle rattles until we do. We're s'pose to be humble while they crawl all over the house, cleaning it with the turtle rattles. Everyone except Oskee, cause he's humble already, but he gets down anyway."

"T-T-Turtle rattles?" I stammered.

"Big ones, snappers, big as a dinner plate, all beaded and the like."

"What's the dream-guessing game?"

"It's not a game." Gramma said. "Earth People believe dreams are real. Between the longest night and midwinter night we remember our dreams. Midwinter night is what Clay People call Groundhog Day..." At that thought she sadly shook her head.

"During dream-guessing we tell our dreams. Elders interpret a dream's meaning, 'guess' we call it, which helps us in the coming year. We believe if we sit on our dreams, don't tell them, we will go mad, crazy. I'm a dream guesser. So is Haksot."

"Can I be here for that?"

"It's not until the last day. I think you'll be home by then."

I sat back on a chair, disappointed.

"So," she said with a sideways glance. "Tell me your dream."

"I had a dream I was inside the hedgerow thicket where you told me not to go, you know? It was fall and I was crunching Sweetgum leaves and all of a sudden turtle rattles slapped my back and I fell in quicksand. An old woman was there in a tree."

Color sapped from Gramma's face. She dropped the meat and grabbed one of the stave chairs, then abruptly sat down.

"Oh my," she said. "She gave you a choice, didn't she?"

I nodded yes and gulped. "To live or die?" I gulped again. "Oh my, oh my. Now you owe her. Now... we all owe her."

"Owe her what?" I asked.

"Nick, go get the old man. Tell him I need him, nothing else."

"It was just a dream, I mean, it wasn't real, was it?"

"Nick, go."

Nick got up somewhat reluctantly and reached for his winter coat on the peg by the door.

Just then there was a knock. Nick opened the door.

My father swung out the storm door, stomped the snow off his feet, and stepped into the warm kitchen.

"Hey, son? Miss me?" He took his hat off, but didn't come any further into the kitchen. "Minnie," he nodded in acknowledgement. Father was one of the few who didn't call her 'Gramma.'

I stood up, glanced at Gramma and noticed her color was back and her features were softer and her eyes were smiling.

"Okay then, let's go home," Father said as Nick ducked out behind him with a forceful closing of the door.

"Stay for supper?" Gramma kinda blurted out.

"Oh, thank you but no. You've done enough."

Gramma's eyes shifted to me. "Get your things. Don't forget your flannels on the chair over there."

"But what about my dream?"

"Not now. Your father's here… *home*. Time to go."

"What's this about a dream?" asked Father.

"I had a dream, I was in quicksand, it was scary, but an old woman…"

"That's enough for now, Hunter. George, your dad, he's had a long trip. Time you got home before more weather comes."

I shut up then, grabbed my things, put on my snow coat and boots, said "Goodbye" to Gramma, and hustled out the door. I didn't want Haksot coming in and calling my father a "goddamn black-coat."

# 6

## *MY FATHER'S HOUSE*

The morning of February 15, 1951, my eleventh birthday, was cold and grey... and cheerless, because I spent most of it sitting rigidly still in the preacher's pew above the organ and across from the seven women and four men that served as a choir for the Bethlehem Unity Evangelical Church.

I was dressed in an acolyte white blouse with bib and a blue skirt and in shoes quick polished one hour before on the shoe polish box in the basement.

At the lectern on my side of the church, my father conducted his chosen scripture. This meant I was behind him and he couldn't see me if I fidgeted or yawned. Not that I yawned that often. I'd learned to stifle them. Yawning always caused someone in the congregation to smirk, which in turn produced a withering glare from Father followed by a dinner table lecture about how my every move reflected on him.

The Bible verse was from Micah. "What does God require? Justice, mercy, and humility." I always liked Micah. He defended poor people, wasn't gooey about love, and none of his prophecies were rants.

During scripture readings I watched the people seated in the pews, and separated the eighty or so average faces into three divisions: 1) Indifferent, 2) Interested and 3) Caring. Caring always polled last, usually in the low teens.

I didn't include Uninterested. I figured the uninterested ones, like my fifteen-year-old cousin Wendell, were present because some other family member forced them to be there.

On that cold February day, Wendell was looking bored as usual on the hard plank pew against the far back wall of the church. My rich Uncle Joe had divorced Wendell's polar-frozen mother, my Aunt Dorothy, six months earlier, about the same time the bull clobbered my mother. Uncle Joe moved south with his girlfriend. He didn't take Wendell with him.

Aunt Dorothy was our church organist. She played as though she was mad at music; as though pounding on the keys with a vengeance would cover the fact that she was angry and unhappy and, in fact, a lousy organist.

Outside the church, Lucinda Eggles had already slipped and cracked her skull on the icy steps leading to the church's front door. Inside we innocently listened to Micah tell us that what we sow is what we reap.

There's no need for ambulance sirens on a Sunday in Bethlehem in February or at any time. The ambulance arrived without fanfare – called by an alert or nosy Ramona Snyder who lived across the street. Ramona was a Seventh Day Adventist – she went to church on Saturdays.

One of the ushers, Carson Bailey, heard voices and felt the commotion. He donned his overcoat and scarf before glancing outside, then shut the vestry door with a loud click. Maybe the loud click alerted my father, or maybe Carson eyeshot Father before the click. In either case, when he finished the scripture reading, and before droning his usual ten-minute prayer, Father leaned over and told me to slip out the side door behind us and go round front and find out what was going on. I was glad to get out of the sanctuary and out of the prayer.

From a hook near the side door I grabbed my faded yellow overcoat and plaid earflap hat, bought for me at Goodwill, and stuck my feet in rubber boots with metal clips, which I left unclipped. Leaning over to clip them in my angel-dress was just too daunting. I wore the boots because I knew from experience Father would grind more thorns into my soul if I ruined my one pair of dress shoes by getting them wet.

It was difficult getting the ruffled choir robe sleeves into the yellow overcoat, so I didn't button the coat. I probably looked like a partially-peeled banana plodding along the snowy sidewalk. I hardly felt protected from the cold.

Mrs. Eggles was on a gurney, moaning. I recognized her even through her blood-caked hair.

Carson looked at me with a 'what are you doing here?' look.

"My dad said to find out what was going on," I whispered.

"Second time this month," Carson said, "but then Lucinda is accident prone."

He called out to the ambulance driver, "Her husband's at home!"

The driver nodded as he and his assistant pushed the gurney into the ambulance. They knew what to do, whom to call. Everyone at Bethlehem's thirty-bed hospital knew Lucinda Eggles and her husband Ray.

Carson pointed at the blood on the icy steps.

"Do you know where the shovel is?" he asked.

I nodded yes.

"Go get it. I better clean this up before Ray sees it, otherwise he might sue. Damn woman. Always late. Likes to make an entrance. Good thing Ray doesn't ever come to church."

"Carson!" called a voice from across the street. "Is she alright? Should I call Ray?" Ramona Snyder stood on her porch in her bathrobe and overcoat and mukluks, curlers in her hair, Sunday paper under her arm. Once again I noticed Ramona finished all her sentences by sticking her chin out like the wicked witch of the west.

At the bottom of the porch steps Ramona's mutt terrier, MacArthur, suddenly recognized me. He knew me by my hat ridiculously perched on my freezing Brylcreemed hair. MacArthur yapped his deranged bark until Ramona called him up on the porch.

I hated that dog.

Ramona lived next door to the grange hall. Between her house and the grange hall was a dirt path that led to the river and then curved into the parking lot behind City Hall. It was my diagonal short-cut on my walk to school, but every time I took it MacArthur would bark and harass me and block the path. One morning I threw stones at him. On that day on my way home from school MacArthur lunged without warning and nipped my ankle. He didn't even draw blood, but I was so angry I took off my hat and swung at him. One of the snaps on a flap hit him in the eye. It must have stung, because he slunk away on three legs while one front paw rubbed the eye.

I never took the grange hall shortcut again. In fact, I didn't even walk down MacArthur's side of the block. Lucky for me he had been trained to stay out of the street.

"No thanks, Ramona!" Carson called back as Ramona shushed the mutt. "The hospital will call. She's fine. Just bumped her head — a little dizzy, that's all."

The church steps were wooden and there was a storage area under the landing. We kept the snow shovel in there. I pulled it out and handed it to Horace, all the while thinking, *It's Wendell's job to shovel the snow. He shoveled the sidewalk. Why did he not shovel the steps?*

"I'll take care of this," Carson muttered. "You go back, tell your Dad everything's all right. She bumped her head is all, the blood..." He pointed at the blood on the icy steps, "It was just a scratch. Scalps bleed a lot."

I knew it was more than a scratch. Scratches don't cause that kind of moaning.

Back inside, I paused at the side door before hanging up the coat and hat and pulling off the boots, grateful for the warmth.

My father was winding down his long prayer "inveighing against traducements" (I told myself to dictionary both those big words.) I slipped silently into my seat during "in Jesus' name, Amen." Father was still at the lectern and, though head-bowed, no doubt felt me return. As the congregation repeated "Amen," he turned and his look questioned, "What happened?"

"Mrs. Eggles slipped on the ice. Hit her head. There was blood. Mrs. Snyder called the ambulance."

"Christ," my father muttered, then turned and nodded at the organist. Dorothy immediately crushed the foot pedal of the organ to the floor and throttled out the opening bars of 'This Is My Father's World,' the unfortunate hymn next in line. I stood and opened the hymnal, wondering if Aunt Dorothy heard me. I knew she didn't like Mrs. Eggles.

'Huffy' was my aunt's word for her. Once I asked Mother what that meant.

"Imperious," she answered.

I had to 'dictionary' both words. Huffy meant annoying; imperious meant arrogant. I thought about that. It seemed to me that 'huffy' described Dorothy better than it described Mrs. Eggles, and while I hated to think of Mother as 'arrogant,' I knew other people in town did.

The hymn ended on a chord with one annoying wrong note. The congregation ungraciously sat down. My father, with pious modesty, rose to the pulpit, drew his black robe and red vestments higher on his shoulders, and assumed his authority to preach.

During the next half hour I first daydreamed methods to use to do away with MacArthur. They involved ropes, burlap sacks, my baseball bat, even a kitchen knife, and all ended with me heaving that yappy mutt into the river.

Then my thoughts switched to my quicksand dream. I had that dream just three weeks prior. My father coming home earlier than expected from his deliverance of my mother to her parents seemed to have messed up a possible ceremony for me. Gramma and Haksot had intended to "doctor me with a burning water lodge," as they later told me, but my father returned me to Bethlehem before that happened. It pissed me off. I'd rather be in one of their ceremonies than be sitting in church in an angel suit.

I thought about what Gramma had told me about Dreaming:

"In Dreaming," she said, "we are shown ancestral openings. Our re-imagined lives can emerge there. Dreaming is so amazing. You don't have to sleep to go there, and dreaming experiences cannot be taken away, because the Source Mind itself never stops dreaming. Dreams never lie. Dreaming is the real world. Everyday life is a caterpillar's cocoon in comparison."

She told us the story about Original Woman; how Original Woman became the Earth Mother, the Master of Our Souls, because she guessed the Dreaming of the Ancient One.

When she finished that story, which took hours to tell, Gramma said, "The reason we have dream-guessing ceremony is simple. Longhouse way we don't separate one person's dream from the whole. One person out of balance means everything is out of balance. Dream-guessing restores balance."

She leaned forward in her sewing chair and stopped her rocking and said: "If we tell our dreams, our dreams can bless our futures. If we do not, holding back can sicken us."

Father served two churches, was chaplain on the reservation, and chaplain at the state hospital. He didn't always have time to write his own material. Sometimes he borrowed his sermons from Harry Emerson Fosdick's Riverside Church radio broadcasts. But the words I heard from him this time dug me out of my reverie.

He was grousing about the Four Horsemen of Calumny. He was using words like slander, defamation, libel and mudslinging.

"Point a finger at someone," he thundered, "you got three fingers pointing back at yourself!"

I dictionaried the word 'calumny' when I got home. It's roughly the same as traducements.

I well knew the unfeeling side of my father: "No, you can't have that. No, we can't afford it. No, you don't deserve it." His stained-glass "no" decrees contradicted his water-color sermons about 'Jesus Is Love.' Their ricochets etched in my consciousness.

That day the windows were covered with frost and Father's words felt exposed and separated, as though someone was pointing a finger at him. My mother? Her father? Unity Church?

I had yet to be told that two weeks previous Mother filed for divorce in a state where adultery, criminal conduct, and abuse were the only grounds.

# 7

## *JUST A DUMB INDIAN*

At the public school in Bethlehem religion played a big role. We pledged allegiance *and* said the Lord's Prayer twice a day. Refugee Jewish kids weren't exempt. On Fridays, cafeteria fish sticks were inevitable and the public school Catholic kids got to leave an hour early to go to catechism class over at the parochial school.

Consequently, Easter week and Spring Break were the same. I was thrilled in late March when Gramma told my father at reservation services on Saturday night that she needed my help, and would my father drop me off at their place for a couple of nights during the week?

Father was reluctant. He wanted me around the house to do spring cleaning chores. But Gramma's will bent his will, and by the way, would I bring a pair of binoculars she knew we had?

"Don't lose them," he had to say to me. "They don't come cheap anymore. I've had them twenty years."

My father took me with him to Jerome Indian School on Wednesday night of Spring Break. I attended Bible class in the Quaker House. It was about the resurrection and stuff.

At the high point in his lecture, he pointed toward the orphanage across the street where the Catholic chapel was. "They preach Christ Crucified," he pontificated, and then more piously, "We preach Christ Risen!" He pointed proudly at the barren cross on our side of the road.

After Bible class, Father tentatively offered to drive us the two miles around to Gramma's house. But Gramma said "no," and made some excuse about "needing to get Oskee settled."

Normally on Wednesdays when Gramma attended Bible class, Oskee and Nick would stay in the dorm overnight so Gramma wouldn't have to get Oskee across the log bridge over Little Ghost Creek and through the fields in the dark. Oskee didn't handle 'dark' very well. This was Easter week. There was no school. Oskee and Nick were already at home. Gramma *wanted* me to walk the back route.

"The moon's near full. We'll be fine."

"Okay," Father said, "but I'll come out here to get him on Good Friday in the morning. We've got noon services. It wouldn't look right, him not being with me for that."

"Of course," said Gramma. "Maybe I'll come too."

It was the first time I had walked that path since my dream about the hedgerow thicket and the quicksand and the vision of a woman who gave me a choice to live or die.

When we passed, just glancing at the dark loom of the thicket, I felt sucking sand tug at me.

"Gramma," I started to say...

"Don't be afraid," Gramma said. "I know this path by heart."

"It's not that."

"I know..."

Through the trees a half-mile distant I could see electric lights from her house. Electric lights meant visitors. That made me nervous.

"What's happening tonight?"

"You'll see."

"I mean, should I be scared?... or worried, sorta?"

"Nothing like that. Different kind of dream tonight. Magical one."

I wasn't comforted by her words. We walked in silence until I felt okay asking what had been dragging on my fear for months: "Gramma, when you said I owed her, and you owed her, what did you mean?"

"Haksot and some other old men are in a burning water lodge right now. They're asking the Spirits that very question, what does she want, why she gave you that choice, what we need to do?"

"Really? Am I s'pose to go in when we get there? When I was here for maple syrup, you said I needed to get doctored in a burning water lodge."

I probably couldn't hide the worry in my voice. It was so like them to have me do something without telling me until the last minute. It was Haksot's thinking. He liked catching me off-guard. He was fond of the expression "Experience is a tough teacher. First she gives you the test and then she gives you the lesson."

"I said the lodge was *for* you. I didn't say you were to go in it. Boys, before their voices change, rarely go into a burning water lodge. They help learn the fire and so on, but don't go in. Nick, he's sitting outside at the door of the lodge, ready to open it and close it. But he won't go in till his initiation days. During maple sap I doctored you for the ague. Remember? Sounds like you put the two together and remembered it your way. Don't be scared."

"I'm not... scared," I croaked.

I had caught flu, 'ague' Gramma called it, when we went to tap the maple trees in early March. It was a cold wet drizzling sleet day. When we brought the sap in for boiling I was burning with fever and hacking at a hot rasp in my throat that wouldn't cough out.

Gramma Minnie had been simmering butternut oil, critical to clumping maple sap into candy. The smell filled the kitchen with sweetness but I was so sick I couldn't have cared less.

Gramma took one look at me and went right to work getting jars of herbs down off the shelves. She brewed a tea of black hemlock root, the gum from some fiery shrub, and lady slipper leaves (not the root) and made me drink it. I shut off my nose and gagged it down. Next thing, thanks to the hemlock, I was in the outhouse cleaning out. When I stumbled back in, they had brought my mat down by the potbelly. I was so sleepy I fell onto it. They told me later that the lady slipper was what knocked me out. While I was sleeping Gramma wrapped a throat-sweat of sage, hops and blue flag, and I slept all night with that hot throat-sweat wrapped tight around my neck.

The next day she made me drink tea from the flowers of purple vervain. Ycchh! Awful, but... I was cured in two days and my father never knew I was sick. Gramma never mentioned it. She knew my blood grandmother had died in the flu epidemic in 1919 and my father feared the flu. If he thought I would get sick like that coming out to the One Knifes', he might never let me come there again.

"Hunter! You listening?"

I snapped out of my recollect.

"Yeah, sorta."

Even though I was walking behind her, she could tell I was daydreaming, or just not paying attention. She motioned for me to walk beside her on the narrow path.

"Believe me," she continued in a confidential way, "you're not ready to go in one of those old men lodges. Spirits are real busy in those lodges. It takes experience to understand. You could get rattled and mentally hurt. That was a powerful dream you had. For us, it's not uncommon for an old one to dream about the Gatekeeper. Fat Face is telling someone to get ready to die. But a young boy and non-Indian to boot -- and she gave you a choice? That doesn't happen." She looked up and said to the sky, "That's never happened!"

I wasn't feeling at ease, and she knew it.

"Hunter, are you scared of us? Did that dream frighten you?"

"Yeah, a little…" I had to be honest. She knows when I lie.

"We are not trying to frighten you. Nobody is forcing you to do things our way. If you choose to stop coming here, that's okay. But I want you to know, we will never make you do something against your will. Never. Please remember that when someone maybe sometime in the future thinks that way."

"Okay," I answered, a little confused.

There was soup cooking on the stove when we got there. Apparently, after every burning water lodge there's a breaking of bread and a thank you prayer that goes with that. The soup was good, even if it was commodity beef and commodity vegetables. The daughter of one of the False Face old men had prepared it. I wasn't surprised. It was normal for women from the same clan to move in and out of each other's kitchens.

The moon was midway down in the west and one day after full. It was chilly but not cold. After we finished eating, Gramma handed me my faded yellow coat and flaptop hat and Haksot told Nick and me to get boots on; we'd be walking in mud. There was no explanation why or where.

We went down the fence line behind the house that kept the calf and two horses out of the peach orchard; crossed the creek, skirted a meadow that was still brown and fledging.

There were two yearling deer foraging the sweet new grass in the peach orchard. The momma dog that came with us did not chase them, nor did they run. I found that remarkable.

Over North where the moonlight faded the orchard into woodlands, I heard the faint but distinct thumping of ruffled grouse wings on an old log. It was late March. In another week there would be as many as fourteen eggs somewhere deeper in the forest. Foxes, snakes, raccoons, mink, rats, and in lean years even humans, would ferret them out. The numbers of grouse had been dropping. I made a mental note to tell Gramma. Maybe she could save them.

Haksot was getting old. He didn't hear the thumping.

He led us to a rocky hummock upslope from a grove of cottonwoods. Forlorn remnants of bark hung in shreds from those trees. It had been a tough winter and the deer had survived by tearing off and eating the cottonwood bark.

On the hummock there were no tall trees and we had a clear view of the night sky.

I had spent hours on my back looking at the night sky in all seasons, but I never knew until then that most migrating birds fly at night and rest during the day. In the old days, on nights of the full moon in spring the Onodowaga clan leaders would count them.

Haksot particularly wanted to count the herons. The Heron clan sat opposite on the circle from the Wolf Clan among the Longhouse People. In the old days the Heron Clan would go out in spring and count wolf pups, but there had been no wolves in New York State in a hundred years.

There was a river of birds crossing the backlight of the moon. I distinguished barn swallows too, but smaller birds were a blur. Haksot pretended to count those with the binoculars. He asked us to keep track of the Herons. Herons are very distinguishable against the moon with their long necks and long tail-feathers, and Nick and I could see them clearly. I counted Herons, but I watched it all in awe.

The moon moved the length of Haksot's long shadow before he said, "The land dwells in us. The stars dwell in the winged ones." It was a signal; time to stop.

On the walk back he told us a story:

"One time long ago the Heron Clan moved to a place that was the territory of a large wolf pack. The Heron Clan knew they could kill all the wolves, but this would change them. They would no longer be a part of the natural order. So the Heron Clan moved on. They kept the balance. In later years, when Wolf Clan people were faced with a critical decision, someone from the tribe would stand up and ask:

"Tell me brothers! Who speaks for the Wolf?" Haksot pointed at the moon, "And someone from the Heron Clan would stand and say, 'We do'."

"In our tribal councils even now the Heron Clan speaks for us, and we speak for the Heron Clan. That's why we still count Herons in spring moon. In the old days the numbers were important. These days it's the experience that counts. It keeps the tradition alive. It widens the path we walk on."

"How so?" asked Nick.

Haksot paused, thinking, and his eyes got watery.

"I'm an Indian. You're an Indian. No one speaks for us. It's not like the old days. In these walled-in times I have to speak for myself. That's not good behavior to my way of thinking. It makes me identify with a narrow path. There's no balance in that, but when I don't speak for myself, the Clay People call me 'just a dumb Indian'."

"If you speak for others, for those less fortunate than you... like Oskee... then you speak for yourself. Oskee needs our help; he is a lesson for us — he teaches us to be human. You speak for Oskee -- you speak for those less fortunate -- you experience being human."

When we got back, Gramma was still awake. She had boiled and cooled eggs and was dyeing them in a jar of elderberry juice. "It's for Oskee," she said.

Haksot picked up an egg, shook his head. "I don't understand Clay People. Rabbits don't lay eggs."

He sighed. "What's that word they like? Seek? Seek and you will find? Doesn't teach a kid how to hunt! We hunt to survive! We don't seek! Seeking is not hunting. Little kids, they go out, look around, and the egg it's there, already cooked, it can't move. It doesn't make sense...

"And that resurrection crap!" He was warmed up. "I die, my body feeds the worms. It don't go floating up to sit on a cloud! Worms feed the green; the green feeds us. It's a circle. It keeps the balance... "

He stood there for a while holding the egg but not looking at it. He looked sad. Then he put the egg down and went off to his room.

"Honσtaɛʔσ:ka tewa'shɛ:h," he said as he left.

"What'd he say?" I whispered to Nick. Nick shrugged, he didn't know.

"Herons," Gramma answered. "He said he only counted twenty herons."

# 8

## *I'LL FEED THE HORSES*

In the barn, hides hung from every wall. Porcupine quills used in sewing, stitching and beading, deer hooves used for rattles, and raccoon stomachs needed for a gambling game were a few of many organic items drying in tightly woven baskets. When the cats caught birds, Haksot saved feathers and skulls. Chickadee skulls in particular were used in divinations.

All the poisonous stuff like hemlock berries, horse-chestnut pulp, and foxglove leaves gathered in the fall were dried in the barn over the winter.

I loved preparing the horse chestnuts. We would build a fire from the leaves and twigs of the tree and then heat the horse chestnuts till they popped. We'd rake the popped nuts from the ashes and pound them into a pulp. The next spring we'd dump the pulp in the shallows of a pond. The poison in horse chestnuts paralyzed bullfrogs. They'd float to the surface. The bullfrogs, still alive but unmoving, were used in the fish traps when the hammerheads, a kind of lake salmon, were running to spawn, usually early April into May.

Haksot literally shoved a peg up the frog's ass. The peg jutted from a trigger paddle, which in turn was attached inside a basket with a trapdoor. By the time we got the traps into the river, the frogs would revive enough to thrash around. They never got free of the peg; however, the thrashing would attract a hammerhead. The hammerhead's bony nose would spark the trigger to the basket door and trap the fish when it tried to swallow the frog.

The horse chestnut pulp was powerful. When we dumped it in one of the shallow ponds in Little Ghost Creek, some of the smaller fish died from it. We couldn't eat the frogs or the fish that had been drugged like that. Haksot said we'd get sick from the poison.

The bullfrogs we ate had to be gigged. We had a short branch from a Bur Oak that had five or more smaller branches at one end. Bur Oak was a solid hardwood that wouldn't snap on impact if we hit a stone or something hard. We cut the branches to form a circular claw and gig the frogs without impaling them. That way they were captured alive and didn't get skewered and ruined. We'd find them by their croaking at night, get down on hands and knees to get close, and then shine them with a flashlight just before gigging them. It was a good lesson in being stealthy and quiet.

Some nights we brought eight or more bullfrogs home in one of those tight woven baskets. Haksot would cut off their heads, gut and skin them, and Gramma would fry them in the big cast iron skillet.

The first time I saw them cooking, it truly startled me. It put the cold queasy in my gut. Those gutted, skinned frogs looked like spread-eagled little humans. Simmering in a fry pan, their leg muscles involuntarily kicked until the hot grease blistered them motionless.

I wondered if I could eat one. I got real self-conscious, looked down, swallowed hard. I felt like the rest of the family was looking at me, wondering how I would react. Looking at those frogs, the words 'yellow' and 'coward' jumped again into my thoughts. Did I have to prove I had courage by eating a frog? My stomach knotted up looking at those frogs frying in that pan, their legs swimming, bumping each other, pushing off, clamoring in the spatter and sizzle of Crisco.

*Sometimes I wondered if my whole reason for hanging out on the reservation was to prove I wasn't a coward.*

Then six-year-old Oskee climbed up on a stool, looked into the fry pan, watched the legs move, and then wailed; held his stomach and wailed as though in grief, until Gramma wrapped her arms around him and turned him away and set him down.

"It's okay, it's okay. It's part of the balance." She looked at me. "Oskee loves frogs. He won't eat them. You don't have to either."

"Yes, I do," I said to myself. "Yes, I do."

Early in June of 1951 when all the saplings were green and full of juice, Haksot and Nick made four ritual trips on horseback up to the ridge, and each time, Nick told me, laid down Indian tobacco and made prayers before they found and cut a perfect branch of Shagbark Hickory.

Then Haksot taught Nick and me how to make a bow. We all sat in the shade in the barn while he worked the bow. It was early morning just days past the solstice.

Haksot made himself comfortable on a stump in a corner and picked up the branch of shagbark hickory that he'd been finishing.

"Shaggy bark holds up – long time – to impact and stress. You always want to work it when it's green and then tie it before it dries. Same with a drum. Hollow cottonwood out green and tie on a skin real tight and let it dry. It won't check that way. Bow won't either once we sweat and oil it."

79

He tried to soften the bow tips with his saliva and shape the gut notches with his teeth, and got nowhere. Maybe if he had more teeth.

"Here," he said handing the bow to Nick. "Bite on that with your side teeth. Crunch down, go easy, once, twice, three times, make a groove."

"The best wood for making a bow is something called Osage Orange. That wood didn't used to grow here. Now they say it does. Some of the men, when they came back from the war, brought it with them."

He took the bow back from Nick, inspected it.

"Your Grampa Tom, when he was stationed in Texas before he went to the war, he learned about that from the Plains Indians he was in camp with. He said you could get sixty pounds of pull out of Osage Orange. They said you needed that on the Plains to kill a buffalo. Of course, Spirit always gives us what we need. With Shaggy bark, if it's a longbow, maybe we get forty pounds. Good enough for a deer. This short one for you, maybe 25. Birds, small four-leggeds, no problem, but you'd have to get very close to a deer to kill it with a bow like this."

He looked at the branch of light-color hickory he had spent days shaping and sanding.

"Anyway, I don't know the songs for Osage Orange. So I stick to what I do know.

"You, Hunter, quit playing with yourself! Sit! Listen! I'm telling you something about hunting. I'm telling you about your name! Keep that up, I'll name you 'Nut-scratcher.'

"Before a hunt we paint to blend in with the forest. Then we stand in smoke and smudge everything, bow, arrows, and clothes to hide our smell. Hands, especially our hands. Smell your hands, go ahead, smell 'em."

We did as we were told.

"What do you smell?"

I shrugged.

"You, you smell *you*! No one else smells like you. You move through the forest, you touch something; your smell is on that plant until the next rain. But that's not the half of it. That plant tells all the other plants for miles around where you are. The plant kingdom; they talk to each other through their juices in their roots and leaves. The four leggeds, they can taste that talk."

He held out his own gnarled hands, looked at both sides. "Our hands say so much about us."

I looked at his hands. With most old men, the face dominates. With Haksot, it was his hands. Haksot's bony, calloused fingers said more than the mole on his chin, more even than the constant wetness in his struggling eyes.

"No one has hands like me, no one's fingerprints match mine. It's the same with everyone," he mused, "and no one's hands touch or suffer the same."

I had watched him braid and twist strands of the inner lining of 'wicopy,' the bark of the leatherwood tree, for the bowstring. His left hand fought to keep the tension. He coursed each of the strands after each twist to take the mock out of them, even though his left hand quivered and his eyes blinked fiercely.

"Grandmother, Grandmother," he said through clenched teeth while coursing the strands.

The bark sinews unraveled six times. Each time he started over with no complaint, only that one-word prayer.

"Hunter!" he barked. "Do you know to always stay upwind, move with the leaves? Do you have that kind of patience?"

"Yeah," I lied.

"Do you know the hunter's stalk, toe-heel, toe-heel? Feel with your toes, not make a sound. Can you walk through a pile of leaves and not make a sound?" he said sharply as he hooked the leatherwood bark string to the bottom end of the bow, noticing without comment that the bowstring loop held fast to the notch Nick had chewed.

"Maybe," I hoped.

"Maybe, there's no maybe... to kill a deer so it doesn't suffer, you have to put the arrow between the first rib and the front leg. That means you have to get in front of it. Very difficult to keep upwind, not make a sound, move with the wind-blown grasses, get in front of a deer. Get in front; the arrow sinks through a lung into the heart. The arrowhead has to be straight up and down or it will break on a rib bone. Do all that, the deer won't suffer and it will taste better.

"To kill a man," he said unemotional, "It takes a soldier, not a hunter. War arrows... the feathers are set so the arrowhead point is sideways. War arrows are for self-defense. You're in a hurry. You don't worry about being quiet. You nock your arrow on the bow by feeling the feathers -- the flat side -- in a hurry while you keep your eyes on the target."

He made the motion of pulling arrows from a quiver and swinging the bow side to side as if shooting at enemies.

"A man will likely die from a shot between his ribs. The higher up," he pointed to his own ribs around his chest, "the less they suffer."

"What if..." I started to say and then regretted it.

His eyes narrowed, "...if you *want* them to suffer, you catch them..." he moved his hand down his side, "under this one. But if you want them to suffer, you're a killer, not a warrior."

He pulled the top of the bow down and strung from the bottom the 'wicopy' he had hand-braided. He grimaced hard and water again was in his eyes. The knuckles on his right hand locked it into a fist as he gripped the bowstring. There was a lot of tension in the wood; it pushed his left hand up so it looked like a claw. He struggled, asked for no help, and finally, grunting, strung the bow.

"No wonder the lazy ones were glad to get guns." He examined the bow again, but his mind seemed elsewhere.

"My son-in-law Tom, Minnie's husband," he said to me and then looked at Nick, "your... Grampa... died at a place they called Iwo Jima. They say he didn't suffer. We never saw the body, only the box. They said, 'Don't look.' We buried him best we could Indian way under the walnut tree by the barn."

He looked at the lingering claw of his left hand and the knuckle-locked fist of his right hand.

"The Gatekeeper," he looked at me, "Fat Face, the one you saw," he paused, "told me Tom would come back in a box."

He wrapped his left claw around the wood shank and hooked the fingernails of his right fist to the bowstring. His body shuddered with pain as he drew the strung bow this first time. Suddenly the knuckles released, his right hand opened, the bowstring thomped.

"I am old," he said, gently kneading his right fingers as he rubbed the back of the left hand against his pant leg. "I don't hunt anymore. My eyes, my ears, can't keep up." He held up his right hand. "My knuckles lock. If I were hunting, the prey would hear the wrath in my hands long before they saw the pain in my face."

He thumped the strung bark again. The wood had stretched out and the sound had a higher pitch.

"This is the way of Creating," he said. "Creating's way brings the high down, lifts the low, takes from those who have, gives to those who have not.

"High and low are in contrast, not in conflict. Remember that. Contrast is the way of the hunt. Conflict is the way of the gun. The way of the gun takes from those who don't have and gives to those who have much."

He pulled on the string again, tested the bow, and seemed satisfied. He wiped the water from his eyes with his sleeve.

"Before a hunt, we sing the Blackface song. We are going to take a life. We draw a picture of the animal in the dirt at the foot of the rock where we paint. We say 'thank you' for the giveaway of the animal we are hunting. The animals know we are coming. Our songs tell them. Our hands tell them." He said the last with a whisper.

At that Nick grunted "ah-huh" to show he was listening. That way was still not second nature to me.

Haksot paused at that and watched to see if I accepted his notion. I was wide-eyed and nodded "yeah."

"Believe me, the animal knows we are coming," Haksot continued. "More than that, they know that they will give away to us, but not without testing us. If we don't measure up, if we can't pass its test, it won't give-away. It takes skill, but it also takes prayer to be a great hunter; gratitude prayers and humility too. Thank that animal for its giveaway before you even start out. You don't do that, any four-legged animal will always outsmart you. Say thank you before you go and the deer will find you before you find it. It's all part of the balance.

"If you hunt with a gun, you don't need a prayer. Guns are the opposite of prayer.

"There's a story we tell," he went on, "about Indians and guns...

"I heard it first from a man named Snow Owl when I was young like you. In those days we couldn't afford bullets, much less guns.

"'Once, many seasons before this time, three Bear Clan hunters spent the Coughing Moon together trapping. They had good fortune. When they brought their furs to the trading post at the end of the season, they had more than enough to buy everything their families needed. There was even enough left over to buy a new rifle.

"One hunter was from the Onodowaga, the People of the Great Stone, our people. Nowadays the white men call us Seneca. How they got Seneca from Onodowaga I'll never know. The second clan brother was from the Onatakeka, the People on the Hills, now called Onondaga. You'd think they'd get Onondaga from Onodowaga, not Onatakeka, but... they're idiots. The third brother was from the Kanyekaono, the People of the Flint, now called Mohawks. Figure that one out!

"So the three Bear Clan brothers there at the trading post, it was easy to divide each families' needs. But who would get the rifle? So they decided. The man who told the tallest tale about hunting would be given the gun by the other two. They asked the man who ran the trading post to be the judge.

"The Mohawk told a tale about his great-grandfather who owned a muzzleloader. The old man never had any lead musket balls so he used cherry pits instead. That was okay for birds, but one time he shot a deer in the head. The deer fell down but then got up and ran away. A year later he was hunting again and had no luck. He saw a cherry tree and decided to pick cherries and get more pits for shot. He was in the tree when it began shaking and threw him out. He looked up and saw that the cherry was growing out of the head between the antlers of a giant deer, the one he had shot the year before.

"Well, that was the Mohawk's tale. Pretty simple, but what can you expect from a Mohawk?

"The Onondaga said, 'That's nothing. One time my uncle was out hunting. He had a rifle but he only had one bullet, so he had to make it count. He came to a stream where he saw a duck swimming. In front of the duck there was a trout breaching for flies. On the opposite bank was a deer. It stood very still because upwind behind the deer was a bear scratching on a tree. My uncle crawled close, took aim and waited. When the trout jumped again he pulled the trigger. His bullet went through the trout, ricocheted off the duck's head, went through the deer and killed the bear. The bear fell on a fox and killed the fox.'

"The Onondaga paused for breath. 'And that fox had a fat rabbit in its mouth.'

"Now only our ancestor, the Seneca hunter, was left. He looked at the other two.

"'One of you take home the rifle,' he said. 'I have no tall-tales about hunting. Seneca hunters never tell tall-tales about hunting.'

"The Onondaga and the Mohawk looked at each other. Then, without another word, the Mohawk handed the gun back to the man from the trading post.

"'Give us back our tail meat,' he said, referring to the delicious marrow found in beaver tails, for which the trader had offered the gun.

"'You keep the gun. We'll keep to the old ways.'

"The Onondaga turned to the Seneca. 'Thank you, brother, for reminding us,' he said."

Nick and I looked at each other. Nick shrugged.

"I don't get it," I said.

Haksot laughed. "We all need tall-tales. Amusements are a need. Feast days, rewards, and blessings are a need. Children are most honest about that need. But I'm talking about the difference between stories and tall-tales. Being willing to turn down that gun, being serious about not telling tall-tales about something as sacred as hunting, as taking a life in order to survive? That makes a story different from a tall-tale."

Haksot thumped the leatherwood string on the bow again, pulled on it, let go, listened to the hum. He scratched at the mole on his chin and then grunted.

"For us, storytelling carries the wisdom of our people and passes it on to the next generation. Stories hold places. Wisdom sits in places. Tall tales *don't* hold places."

He unstrung the bow and handed it to Nick. His hands were laughing.

"The lives of most people are tall-tales. We tell them for entertainment. But sometimes, not often, one man or one woman represents the people. Then they become legends, like that ancestor that chose the bow over the gun."

He stood, adjusted his pants, pulled down on the crotch.

"You two go build a burning water fire. Sixteen stones. Put the bow on the altar. We need to steam it, seal in the spirit of the hunt."

Nick and I both looked towards the corral.

"Go, build a fire," the old man said. "I'll feed the horses."

# 9

## *LET 'EM BE CATS*

The front door faced the sunrise, not the road. It opened into the kitchen from a porch with planks so worn square-head nails (that's how old the house was) were sticking up out of the wood. In the summertime walking barefoot we learned to avoid them; otherwise they would cut our feet. We'd pound them back in with the hatchet, but they'd poke up again in no time.

The first thing I'd look for walking in the door is whether red cedar nettles smoldered in a Studebaker hubcap on a metal shelf above the stove. If not, I'd replenish the coals in the hubcap and then put more cedar nettles on the coals. It was important to keep that aroma going. The smoke that wafted from the cedar spiritually cleansed the air of two spirits that Gramma called 'Ojihaya! -- Devil's Songs' and 'Onowatko -- Corn Bug Dancers.'

Dominating the kitchen was the stove with its stovepipe jutting out the north-facing wall. A cast iron skillet that needed a foot of space and a smoke-blackened coffee pot held squatter's rights to two of the iron hot plates.

Opposite the stove was the opening to the parlor. The door was long gone. The heat from the kitchen helped keep the parlor warm, although there was an old stone fireplace on the west wall that did get used in winter. A hand-tied rug, a big red Pullman sofa, family pictures on the walls, a few raggedy upholstered chairs, and – believe it or not – an out of tune upright piano made up the furnishings.

Two doors on the south wall led to two bedrooms, Gramma's and Haksot's. I never went in Haksot's and only rarely had I been in Gramma's room, but I did know that she had a commode for middle-of-the-night wintertime use. I wouldn't be surprised if they told me Haksot had a bucket. It wasn't something I considered asking, although more than once I heard him complain that he didn't "have a pot to piss in or a window to throw it out of."

Since I never went in his room, I didn't know if it had a window or not.

Just to the right of the opening to the parlor were stairs to two tiny gabled rooms on the second floor. They were Nick and Oskee's rooms. I either slept on a pad on the floor in Nick's room or on the Pullman sofa in the parlor when I stayed over. Those stairs were really narrow, steep and with a scuff-groove in the middle of each step.

At the wall opposite the porch door was a double sink and a hand pump that drew water from the well. It only took seven pumps to draw water. The water table was less than thirty feet. I thought a hand pump that pumped water into a sink inside a house was smart. At the cottage I was always hauling buckets from an outside pump, rain or shine.

Beside the sink was the door to a covered plank walkway to what had once been a four-hole outhouse, but was now a two-seat toilet that flushed into a septic tank with its own electric water pump.

"Someday," Gramma kept saying, "we'll build out to it and we'll have inside plumbing! In the meantime, it's still an outhouse!"

Against the south wall was an old icebox, the kind that had the motor in a basket on top. There was a kerosene lamp on the table and another on the sideboard in the corner near the front door, even though the One Knifes had electricity.

"FDR gave it to us," she liked to say. They had electricity, but not the money to use it all the time. The electricity primarily pumped water for the farm animals on days the windmill didn't turn and/or kept food cold in the old icebox and the meat locker and milk cooler in the barn, and to pump water to the flush toilets.

In the wintertime they ran a few light bulbs if the kerosene ran out and she couldn't "borrow" any from 'St.' Jerome. In the summertime we took baths in sun-warm rainwater in an old horse trough in the garden, or we went swimming at the Indian swimming hole at the river. In the winter the family bathed at the Indian School.

Nick and I kept the wood box next to the stove filled with foot-long splits of tamarack and possumwood branches. Both were hardwoods that burned a long time but had enough inner oil to kindle from coals. I chopped possumwood branches with a vengeance. I loved being trusted with a hatchet. We also brought in hickory. Hickory charcoal, made two to four weeks after a green-cut, was best for smoking venison into jerky.

Around the middle of June, when the strawberries hung from the vine, was when the healing herbs were gathered for the coming year. For four days the 'old ways women' fasted and prayed and then hunted the forest for healing herbs. The women would go to the edge of the forest and make an offering of Indian tobacco and corn meal and then shake 'deer toes' rattles.

Gramma told me a little-person spirit, called Jokoa, like an elf but really little, the size of a man's thumb, would appear and guide them. Jokoa knew who would be sick in the coming year and what herbs would be needed. The women would pick the herbs Jokoa indicated.

When the women returned, everyone on the reservation had a great feast they called 'strawberry time.' For four days we ate strawberry shortcake with fresh cream morning, noon, and night. Strawberries, because they are shaped like a human heart, were considered to be sacred.

"They keep your heart strong," Gramma said.

During summer and fall there were herbs and baskets of vegetables and fruit drying from ropes and racks in every room -- sassafras and peach blossoms and mint along with the more bitter nettles, fennel, poke roots, horse garlic, and dandelions. Strawberries, blackberries, and elderberries simmered into preserves on the stove. The air had a 'feel' to it, a 'texture' unqualified and navel.

Year-round, coffee simmered in its pot, red oak bark steeped in a kettle on the potbelly, and white willow bark used to relieve headaches and tooth aches mellowed in cool water by the door.

Once I cut a finger with a knife that was tainted with rotten meat. My finger turned black. Ginseng root, indigo, basswood bark taken when the False Face masks were carved on the tree, and root of moonwort blended into petroleum jelly from the Oil Springs Reservation made a salve that drew out every kind of poison, from bug bites to snakes. Gramma put the salve on my finger and the next day it was white and a day later normal. I never forgot that.

Foxglove, sawdust from a pitch-pine knot plus the tops of a certain kind of poppy soaked in two quarts of homemade elderberry wine was a heart medicine. Haksot strained out all the sawdust and other gunk and poured the wine into glass bottles. He drank this concoction every day. I tried it once. It was foul tasting. It ruined elderberries for me, which was too bad because elderberries were also held in high regard. Never mind the colonists brought them here. After two hundred years Indians all over the East Coast had made elderberries theirs.

All parts of the elderberry plant were used. In July and August we picked clusters and clusters of the small berries, dried them on the drying floor, then cooked them into a rich sweet sauce and preserved them. Sometimes Oskee ate pancakes spread with those preserves and nothing else for a week at a time.

A wash made from the stems made a very deep black dye. Haksot showed Nick and me how to straighten green elderberry branches with our teeth and make bird arrows. We hollowed out larger branches with heated skewers, then bored holes on top and made flutes and whistles. Nick and I also quickly learned hollowed-out elderberry stems could be blowguns or spit guns, which in turn got us plotting against Father Justus. The pith we bored out was dried and used as tinder for bow drills and for flint and steel. Stems were also used in a bow drill.

Summers, Gramma attached a cotton ball dipped in ether to the screen on the porch door. That and a big stinky helped keep the flies away. She allowed the big stinky to work its magic by the outhouse.

Thanks to the flies, no-see'ums, gnats, and moths Gramma never let us take down spider webs. Even so, Nick and me stood at the screen door and swatted flies for an hour during an afternoon. We both loved doing that and competed to see who killed the most.

Everywhere outside was the smell of farm: one fattening hog, chickens by the dozen, two horses, a calf, rabbits and dogs and cats. The farm animals that were raised for food were never named. Dogs and cats were not allowed inside the house. They slept in the barn or outside in summer and under the house in winter.

The three dogs were Airedales, bred on the rez and very popular even though they originally came from England. Haksot liked that breed because they stalked and chased wild animals instead of just barking at them, yet properly trained left the farm animals alone. They kept raccoons and foxes out of the henhouse, rabbits out of the garden, warned off snakes, and protected Oskee when he was outside.

Cats, as many as a dozen in summertime, all feral and never named, killed rodents in the barn and birds in the garden. Gramma would put food out in winter for both dogs and cats. I thought it was okay to try to get close to one of the cats until Haksot stopped me.

"They got a job to do. You start petting them, putting them on your lap, they turn into pussies." He grinned. "Just leave 'em be cats."

# 10

## *PLACE HAS MEANING*

In mid-July, Oskee's mother Norma lost her job or something and ended up back on the reservation. Some nights she'd come in from wherever she was and flop on the couch in the parlor. Other nights she never made it out of the back seat of her beat-up '41 Hudson.

Near the end of the month, the Hudson stopped running and so did Norma. She spent a week sitting in the parlor shaking and shivering as if it was winter. Gramma doctored her with alternating doses of alder bark, ginseng, and poplar bark teas.

"She's drying out," Nick confided, "but don't tell anyone I said that."

I didn't. I liked Norma and I knew what 'drying out' meant.

The first two weeks of August I spent at Camp Mission Hill on the north shore of Lake Chautauqua. I was sent there because our church's president had sent his son Billy there the year before and, I don't know, that seemed to be the reason I should go. Maybe the church president paid for it. That would be reason enough for Father.

Mission Hill turned out to be a Bible camp. Campers spent a good portion of every day in the mess hall listening to some wackadoo try to 'save' us. The Bible Thumper wanted at least one convert from every morning and afternoon session. Other guys would go up to the front of the hall and pretend to be saved just so we all could get out of there and carry on with the normal camp activities like swimming or canoeing on the lake. I never opted for salvation myself. The wackadoo reminded me too much of Father Justus. Fortunately there were enough volunteers.

I wasn't saved but while I was there a tick burrowed into the very tip of my wiener. I wasn't bothered by it. Ticks are a fact of life in the country. I got ten or more a summer and would just snap them off, leave the head in, and then put Gramma's salve on the welt. Since I didn't have any salve with me and since my wiener is not a good place for an infection, I didn't snap off that tick's head.

Instead I went to the nurse, a 'Mother Goose' look-alike who I guess was either the Bible Thumper's wife or sister. She had the same last name. Well, when I whipped out my wiener to show her the tick, she shrieked like a stuck pig in barbed wire. She then recoiled near-faint when I took a step closer. She was so prissy she wouldn't touch that tick. She wrapped me in a blanket and took me to a doctor in Mayville to get it out. I don't know what her problem was. Maybe it was because the tick was bloated so full of blood she couldn't see its legs wiggle anymore.

Father told me later he was sorry he sent me to that camp. He said he had no idea that the place was a salvation center, but honestly I didn't believe him. He sent me there because the timing was good. He needed to park me somewhere while he was doing his counseling training. That year, 1951, he spent the whole month of August at the University of Rochester taking classes from some guy named 'Gestalt.'

The last two weeks of August and the first week of September I spent on the reservation at Gramma Minnie's. We didn't have the cottage anymore. My father sold it for $600 cash to some "suspicious looking guy," so he said, in order to help pay my mother's hospital bills and because of the bad memories. Mother was in Pennsylvania living with her parents. She had written several times asking me to come visit, but I had no desire to go there.

That same summer Nick spent the whole month of August in Buffalo with *his* mother. Mavis seemed to have gotten her life together, worked at the Veteran's Hospital, had an apartment and a car. Norma said she heard Mavis had "kicked out her fat guappo (whatever that was) boyfriend," and joined an Episcopal Church.

While Nick was gone Norma slept in his room. By late August I guess she was dried out. She began acting and looking natural, except for the throwing up in the mornings. The nights I was there, I slept on the couch in the parlor. Those mornings I would hear Norma at the sink vomiting, then pumping water and rinsing her mouth out and sometimes vomiting again.

I heard Gramma's voice then too, soothing the words "go for the medicine before it's too late." Usually when Gramma said the word "medicine" she was referring to plants. I knew she had plants for upset stomach. I wondered what was different about Norma's situation.

One morning I heard Norma say, "I was raped, Momma. I didn't intend for this pregnancy, I was raped. Do the spirits give medicines for that?"

"The spirits have medicines for the sick," is all Gramma said.

Nick came home changed by his month-long visit with his mother. He acted moody and resentful and he frowned and scowled whenever asked to do chores or keep an eye on Oskee. Usually he was glad to come home, so that made me question.

"What's wrong?"

"None of your business."

"But…"

"Stay out of it."

Labor Day we were all sitting on the porch in the twilight watching the fireflies emerge in the peach orchard and listening to the crickets in the weeds around the house tell us the temperature. Gramma rocked in her rocker, Nick sat on the planks near her feet whittling a cottonwood branch. I leaned under the oil lamp against one porch roof column reading a book. Norma sat leaning on the opposite column puffing on a Chesterfield. Between us on a step Oskee played with wooden animals. Haksot sat on a hand-hewn log bench drinking his heart medicine, elderberry wine.

Every so often Norma would swat at mosquitoes buzzing her ear or biting her neck. The rest of us had rubbed on some grisly mixture of burdock root, petroleum jelly, and horse garlic. The mosquitoes pretty much left us alone. Norma refused it.

"I don't wanna smell like a 'Dago.'"

She stole a sly smirking look at Nick when she said that. Nick shot back a look that burned with anger. Those two looks put a bad taste in my mouth that I didn't understand, but I still blurted out: "What's a Dago?"

Norma snickered, "Where'd you get this kid?"

Gramma glared at her daughter.

I hid from Norma's snicker by digging my eyes into the book I was trying to read under the weak light of an oil lamp.

It hurt me inside to be scorned by Norma. It hurt 'cause she was so pretty, like Miss Elman and like my mother once was. Norma was set-on-fire, twenty-four years good-looking, especially in the lamp's flickering shadows. 'Dried out,' the dark circles under her eyes were gone and her honey-amber skin color had returned. She had golden cat-eyes, glossy raven hair, and… *that skin.* She was as sultry as the close humid air that swaddled us. I so wanted her to like me.

She sat there smoking and watching her son Oskee play with a wooden frog Nick carved out of cottonwood. Her dress had hiked up over her knees. She caught me looking over the top of my book at her legs. Her cat-eyes sparked and she didn't bother to push her dress down. Instead, she put her breasts to her knees, looked at me and purred, "You do know how to whistle, don't you, Hunter?"

I was tongue-tied, dry-mouthed struck dumb.

Gramma barked, "Norma! He's ten years old! Daughter, don't you ever let up?"

Norma giggled with shaded joy, and then innocently cooed, "You don't like my Lauren Bacall imitation?"

Gramma just scowled.

Gramma and Norma had been pitting cherries for canning, but they stopped when it got too dark. Gramma just rocked in her rocker. The rocker legs made that whump-whump heartbeat sound and the plank porch floor creaked under the motion. It was most reassuring.

Haksot was unusually quiet that night. Usually he'd lecture, teach, or just gripe, especially if he had more than two cups of wine. He'd sit with one hand atop his walking stick and the other hooked to the cup on his knee. The pitcher of wine was on the bench beside him. Gramma's rocker was next to the bench and she tried to keep him to two cups, but didn't always succeed.

I read books or magazines until the light fell. My mother had made me read a book a week when she was around and it was a habit I happily kept. No one in the One Knife family ever read outside of school. Probably Haksot didn't know how. Still, they didn't *seem* bothered by my need.

The family was 'on-edge,' quiet. I put my book down and looked around. They all seemed dug into their thoughts, so I tried counting cricket chirps. Count how many in 14 seconds and then add 40; the sum is the temperature. I gave up, though. It's impossible to count seconds and chirps at the same time. No one owned a watch. The clock in the parlor was only right twice a day.

Haksot was so quiet, so lost in thought it disturbed me. I wanted him to get talking, tell a story or something. I dug out a question that had been on my mind:

"Haksot, one time you said that wisdom sits in places. What did you mean?"

He didn't respond. Didn't look at me.

I cleared my throat and raised the volume. "Haksot, one time…"

"I heard you the first time," he growled, then picked up his coffee cup wine glass, drained it, and set it down hard.

"Look, it's simple. Wisdom for your people is in books, for us in its places. We identify with the land, with places, by our senses, not by ideas. A book can't hear, taste, sniff, feel, see. A place can. The land can. Understand?"

There was an undertone in his voice that scared me a little. Normally he was eager to talk, even if he had nothing to say.

I held up the book I was reading. It was Richard Halliburton's *Complete Book of Marvels*. "This book is about places. This guy traveled all over the world and wrote about the most amazing adventures. He jumped into a grotto in Mexico and snuck into Mecca."

Haksot shifted his weight and leaned forward on his cane.

"So what!! Words, 'specially English words, are not the same as places. This guy – when he wrote about a place, did he talk about how the wind feels, or how the heat moves day to night, or the texture of the rain; which color is the deepest, what's the strongest aroma, the loudest songbird? Every place has a Soul Fire. Did he mention the Soul Fire in the places he went?"

"Haksot!" Gramma said quietly but in her warning voice.

Haksot spread his hands and looked at her with innocence in the middle of his eyes and a wink playing at the corners.

"Places have Soul. The Soul of a place, I leave it in the language of the place. English words shuffle the Soul of a place like it's a deck of cards! I'm not tellin' him not to read. I'm talkin' about how place is different from words. Experiencin' a place and writin' about a place ain't the same."

This was not the story-telling voice I knew. It put me off-kilter and defensive. I tried holding my ground with: "What he writes about makes me want to go to all those places. He calls places 'marvels.' He's an explorer. He writes about what he does."

"What *he* does... not what the *place* does. That's my point. What's yours?"

Feeling under attack, my voice choked and I squeaked: "So what's wrong with that?"

"Nothing's wrong with that." Norma spit a piece of tobacco off her lip. "Mom, better take the pitcher away, he's starting to lecture on us."

Haksot turned and actually snarled at her, "Which way is the wind blowin', Norma?" That was his expression. That was his way of saying, 'Who asked for your two cents?'

"From the south, Old Man." Norma fired right back. "And the toads must be out because the crickets' song changed."

"The song changed 'cause they're done mating. They're all laid back now, same as you, smoking cigarettes."

Norma didn't answer, just took a drag on her cigarette, made an 'O' circle with her lips and tongue-clucked three smoke rings at Haksot.

I didn't feel the wind, and I noticed no change in the crickets' songs. The sarcasm in Norma's voice and the unforgiving tone in Haksot's I did notice. I looked at Nick and saw he was smiling, but keeping it close. Nothing new there. He kept everything close.

I followed his eyes and looked up. The wind was from the south. It gently rustled the top of the huge elm under which Norma's beat-up Hudson was now permanently parked. I saw three, maybe four bats swooping around up there. The upstairs wind must have brought a swarm of mosquitoes.

Haksot was watching me. When I looked back at him, I dropped my eyes. I saw tears I didn't want to see forming where the wink had been. I felt lost; I didn't understand the emotions around me, and that made me feel unimportant.

"You asked about wisdom, how wisdom sits in places. I was getting to that before I was interrupted," Haksot grumbled. "In the old days when the people first came to a place, they studied how the place lived. They studied what was done *by* a place. More important, they looked at what a place *does not* do. From that they understood their chances for survival in that place."

*How does a place not do something,* I wondered.

"Does the red fox birth three or six pups? Three pups, hard year comin'. Do the bears come out of their dens when the maple sap flows or do they wait until the lily blooms? The Earth tells a bear if spring will be early or late, and what food is available and when. And that in turn tells us. Earth never lies. Never...

"Wisdom sits in places 'cause places have Souls. In the stones in those places is memory of a world where our ancestors were in harmony with everything on Earth. There is a great stone at the head of Seneca Lake. We call it the Place-Holding Stone. Nowadays that's translated as 'Story-Telling Stone.' No matter..."

*I knew about that. I had read a book of Seneca Stories by a guy named Fenton and one of the stories was about the orphan boy who heard the Stone talk and saved the origin stories for the people.*

"Every year in November we climb that Stone, do ceremony; honor where wisdom sits. When events confound us, we go there and travel in our minds on the tracks of our ancestors. We call out the stories that got done long ago; the stories that teach us how to live, tell us what to do. Maybe this year," he looked at Nick, "we will take the two of you there."

*That made me feel better. Maybe I wasn't unimportant.*

Gramma stopped rocking, put her hand up like she was in school. "Names have meaning, too. Our ancestors were flint-knappers. In one try they made a knife sharp as steel. Found the right piece, studied the grain and the veins, knapped it with the tip of a deer antler. One pass. Perfect. So, we got our family name, One Knife. And that talent, flint-knapping, shows up today in Nick, the way he can carve wood. He has a gift."

She looked affectionately at Nick. Nick looked back, but didn't seem to care. I realized Gramma was trying to make him feel better. He had been in such a bad mood.

Norma lit one cigarette from the end-coals of the last one, then smoothed her dress back over her knees; maybe responding to the way Gramma was softening the sharp emotions in the air.

Gramma kept talking, smoothing: "Nick, his Indian name, Onikwa:oneta, means 'Corn Hill.' That's a powerful name; it's a place where corn grows to fourteen feet. It's blessed. The whole tribe once got their seed corn from those plants. The county, though, they said that his real name was confusing so they shortened it to 'Nick' and his mother went along and it's in the records that way."

"That reminds me…" the old man said abruptly. He shook his cane at Nick.

"What?" Nick snapped back.

"Tomorrow, you and Hunter go down to the creek to that place below the dam where they dredged all that rock. Bring back as many perfect round pebbles as you can find, little ones, you know, like we use in a rattle. On the way back, above the dam there's a marsh. Look around on the edges for wild gourds. We'll dry some, make rattles, we'll make a rattle for Oskee. Take the dogs. That's heavy brush gettin' there and there'll be rattlesnakes out."

"Do we have to? Can't it wait?" Nick sounded downright rude.

"End of summer, water is low. Perfect time. I'd go but… there's berries to pick."

"Where is the Corn Hill? Is it a place where wisdom sits?" I felt shoved aside again so I tried to interrupt.

Nick got my attention, shook his head and pointed at Haksot. Haksot was leaning to the left. That meant he had to fart. Usually he would thump his cane on the planks and rip one out, but this one pooped out like a wet-fart.

He pushed up off the bench with his cane and turned for the outhouse mumbling, "Goddamn gettin' old."

Norma also stood up. She stamped her foot on the planks next to Oskee. He looked up and she signed in the back-porch, country homespun sign language the family created for her deaf son.

"C'mon, it's time for bed." She signed actions. "Go. Pump water at the basin, wash up. I'll help you."

Norma turned to Gramma as Oskee obediently headed inside.

"If you take Oskee to work tomorrow, I'll go with the boys. If there's a marsh, I'll look for the…" she glanced at me. "…You know, those plants."

Something told me to look away from her and watch the dogs. They were slanting across the grass between the barn and us. Even in the darkness, by their attitude I could tell the hair on their neck was raised. Something near the henhouse had their nostrils twitching.

Gramma probably nodded. "In the morning I'll show you what to look for. Take tobacco and make an offering. Say a prayer for help. Don't hide what you're doing or be ashamed; you lose your focus. You got leggings or high boots? It's rough country."

"Damn." Norma took one last draw off her Chesterfield, dropped then stubbed her cigarette on the plank beside Nick.

Nick scowled, took his whittling knife and stuck it angrily through the butt into the plank, then got up and gestured to Gramma.

"Well, then why doesn't *she* just go? She can find the stones as well as I can."

I had never seen Nick so resentful. What was going on?

"There's no shade below the dam. It's gonna be real hot tomorrow. And Oskee already has a rattle. If she's goin' anyway…"

"Nick, what's wrong?" Norma sounded contrite.

Nick didn't answer. He just glowered at Norma.

Gramma soothed, "I know it's hard for you to understand, but we need for you to do this."

Nick stood stone still, fist clenched. To disobey Gramma went against everything he knew.

"I'm sorry, Nick." Norma reached down and pulled the stuck knife out of her cigarette butt. "Tell you what. Take your new bow. Try it out." She handed the knife to Nick shank-end first.

"No animals will be out in this heat." I noticed he flattened the knife against his leg, blade safe. "Especially below the dam."

"We'll find persimmons! We'll pick persimmons too while we're out there." Norma was determined. "Nick, I… have to go… these medicines… they're… and you know the way."

"You need medicine and I know the way. My gettin' stones is a trick just to take you there. Just like mom said…"

Nick blinked back tears. His fingers closed around the shank. He gripped the knife like a weapon.

Alarm sounded in Gramma's unusually loud voice. "The stones are not a trick! We need the rattles for the ceremony! They have to be new, everything new." She reached out to grab Nick's hand but Nick pulled away. "Nick, talk to me! What is it? What did your mother say to you?"

Nick waved Gramma away, started for the door, then turned back and looked at her. The conflict and pain on his face was serious. There was something he didn't want to ask, but he did want to know. He struggled, but finally asked: "Gramma, are you a witch?"

"A witch?... you mean, like with the broomstick and pointed hat? What makes you think that?" She started rocking again, but the whump-whump sound didn't cover the trouble.

"You're gonna do a ceremony with rattles, scare away evil spirits, right?"

"Leave it to Mavis," Norma groaned.

"Norma, shut up. You've said enough for one night."

"Damn again..." Norma said under her breath.

I was so surprised I involuntarily stood up. This family was sounding like any other family to me, and why... was it because I asked a question about wisdom?

"Does your mother think I'm a witch?" Gramma tilted her head back as she asked.

"She said that people say you're a witch."

"Ahhh... people say... That word witch; it's from the time of the missionaries. They used 'witches' and 'evil' in the same breath. They feared the women in our tribe, because in our way clan mothers make all final decisions. The missionaries called us 'evil witches' and killed a few of us over time. Your mother has separated from her heritage and her family and now she's using words like 'witch' to separate you."

She stopped rocking, pushed off from the chair arms, stood up very firmly, her stature filled with power. I had never seen her so impressive; suddenly she was all medicine-woman like. Norma actually shrank back.

"I am 'Kahastesha.' I am a nature person." She looked directly at Nick. There was unease in his eyes. I know there was nervousness in mine.

Gramma continued in that authority-voice I'd never really heard before: "I have learned to harness certain powers, plant powers. I can *see* and sometimes I use what I see to cause change, but *only for good.*" She shook her index finger sharply. "There is no clear English way of explaining how I do that. But believe it, this is the way it is."

She gazed towards the elm tree, but she was looking at more than the elm tree.

"My grandmother was a very great Kahastesha. She taught me how to talk to the plant nations. She taught me that the plant world, the 'green,' is the wisest beings on the Earth. Why? Because they take care of the place where they live and they save it for future generations. After the plant nations come the animals, and then us. And we are far behind. Humans, it's a constant struggle... very few of us save the Earth where we live for our offspring. Families fall apart... that was unheard of in the old days...."

Gramma looked at Norma and then back at Nick and she softened and the 'Gramma' in her came back.

"Be kind to Norma. Help her tomorrow. She not only needs the medicines in those plants, more than that she needs the wisdom in them."

Gramma sat back down, clenched the arms of the rocker, and lapsed into a reverie.

"Mavis was seventeen when Nick was born. I took care of both for the next five years. Then she ran off with some guy. Another five years. Now he's gone and she's alone. She's ready to be a mother. My goodness."

There was a prolonged silence. Nick was holding the knife loosely by the handle, the point straight down. I worried he would drop it into his bare left foot. I shuffled my feet and looked away, feeling once again like an outsider and wondering if this family was falling apart; this family that I so desperately wanted to be a part of, and was any of this my fault...?

Finally Nick cleared his throat with effort, "I'm sorry Gramma." His lower lip quavered, "It's just that... she's my mother... she wants..."

"I know what she wants. I just wish she did her wanting with gratitude. Go, wash up. Tomorrow you help us and then you decide. Maybe you will decide to live with your mother for good. If I were an evil witch, you would not have that choice. The point is: Kahastesha are not evil! Go, wash up now, cool off."

Norma had gone around, opened the screen door, glanced in and apparently saw Oskee was all right.

"C'mon, Nick. I'll pump water on your head. I always loved that on a hot day when I was little. You can sleep in your bed tonight. I'll sleep with Oskee."

Norma and Nick went inside. After the door closed, I heard her apologize again.

"I'm sorry for what I said about... you know... Dagos... I'm sorry."

I didn't hear what Nick answered, and I still didn't know what a 'Dago' was and why Norma was apologizing.

What I did know at that moment was that I was not really a part of this family.

Gramma began rocking again. I felt like a fly on the wall, tense, waiting to duck another swatter. Even so, Gramma heard my thought-mind.

"Hotka... one who is evil is called 'Hotka,'" she said absently.

"Isn't that... the name of the little people?" I thought out loud.

"No, that's Jokoa. Interesting, hmmm, that you reflected that." She gazed at me as though looking into me. "You're such a puzzle to us. We didn't expect you in our lives. The gatekeeper, she changed all that."

"What gatekeeper?"

"The woman you saw, Fat Face. She's a gatekeeper."

"What's that mean?"

"Hoo Nellie." She shook her head. "Gatekeepers are guardians at thresholds. She protects the Lodge of the Ancestors. She also tests our commitment."

"Commitment? To what – like, to what it takes to be a nature person? Is Nick gonna be that?"

From inside the house the pump handle squeaked.

"Nick is Fire, like his mother. Fan a fire, it flares up." She looked up over my shoulder. "Haksot is Earth." I looked behind me, expecting to see the Old Man, but there was only the distant scuttle of dogs chasing something.

"What's the difference between Earth and Nature people?"

"That's a good question. Earth people, they read what's outside; animals, stones, the wind, like that. Nature people, we're in the center. We 'see' natural law outside but we 'read' it with all our senses inside. For instance, we 'read' that illness comes from resisting natural law, resisting change, maybe… resisting ourselves."

She paused considering her next words.

"Natural law means 'all things change.' Change requires each of us to adapt or transform or be left behind. That's where the wisdom of the plants comes in. They work on the resistance to change. A 'Kahastesha' knows which plant."

Again she looked over my shoulder. "Stories too. Stories, especially ones from the land, teach us how to adapt and live with change."

"What am I? I mean like fire, earth…?"

"You're a water person. You're a way-finder. It's good you see Nick struggle. One day his experience will help you decide what to do when your mother comes for you."

Those words stopped me. Every time I thought of my mother I felt guilty. I feared I had caused the accident with the bull and I feared my mother blamed me. I couldn't live with that feeling all the time. I didn't want my mother coming for me.

"Is my mother a water person?"

Minnie One Knife rocked for many long seconds, whump-whump, whump-whump, whump-whump, before answering.

"I don't know her well enough to say. From what I've heard, she resists joyfulness and happiness. We call that 'the water sickness' – melancholy, disconnection, depression. When you are older, when your voice changes, there's a water initiation ceremony you can do. Otherwise, maybe you suffer the same as your mother. The spirits in the burning water lodge suggested we teach you, prepare you for that. Water Spirits line up connections and dislodge what's stuck. It's a powerful experience, and it will take commitment."

"And it will take time," said a voice behind me. It was Haksot, emerging out of the darkness. "We can't cut corners. We've never done that for a Clay Person before."

He sat back down on the bench, squirmed a little.

"Tomorrow, you bring me a stone, too. A bigger one, like we use in the lodge. Pull it from the creek, you hear? From *in* the water. The stone you bring back tomorrow, I'll read it and we'll see."

The talk of Mother 'coming to get me,' then the water ceremony which somehow felt scary, and then Haksot blunt as the stones he reads – I was getting twitchy and sweaty.

Gramma noticed, "Best you wash up now. Cool off. Sleep on the sofa tonight. Leave Nick alone with his thoughts and dreams."

I picked up my book about 'marvelous places,' and reached over to turn down the flame on the oil lamp. There was a big school of 'no-see-ums' swarming the light.

"Gramma, you said the plants are the smartest, then the animals, then us. What's dumber than us… bugs?"

"Missionaries," Haksot said abruptly, "they're insects too."

The planks creaked and the rocker whumped. I stopped at the screen door to hear her answer.

"Well," she laughed, "certainly people who do evil, hurt others, do harm to the Balance. They're not just dumb, they're stupid."

When I entered the kitchen I noticed there was no cedar burning in the Studebaker hubcap. As I filled it with coals from the stove and tossed on some more cedar, I heard Haksot ask: "Nick gonna leave?"

"He'll live with Mavis for a while. It's right. He stays here, the resistance builds; one day makes him sick."

"What about the preacher's kid?"

"He's water. He'll take the path of least resistance."

Haksot sighed, "The old ways are all sung out, Minnie. Barely an echo is left. Mavis, Norma, now Nick. They don't care."

"They care... they do." She paused. "They just don't understand how the old ways can help them in today's world... cars... atom bombs... wars thousands of miles away, and radios and that thing called television. Does the Great Stone have stories for that? I'd like to believe it does."

There was a quiet moment and I strained to hear her say, "He has a Place of Emergence. I've seen it in his heart. We're supposed to teach him, but they haven't shown me the reason why."

"Kahsah, a Clay kid... who woulda thunk it... ?" Haksot sounded unhappy.

"Who indeed..."

Gramma kept rocking, but the whump-whump sound was no longer heartening.

# 11

## *WHOLENESS HAS A TEMPERATURE*

In October 1951, an art exhibition by a guy named M.C. Escher was touring the country. He was some famous artist who only became known in the United States following World War II. Reproductions of his art on display in a New York City museum appeared in a Sunday New York Times. A Bethlehem banker got a dozen copies of the Sunday Times delivered to the train station early every Monday morning. He distributed them to a select few around town, my father included.

October 1951 was also the year Bobby Thompson put the Giants in the World Series with his three-run homer in the ninth inning off Ralph Branca. Walking home from school that day, I heard Russ Hodges on Mutual Radio screaming: "The Giants win the pennant, the Giants win the pennant!" It was coming from the fire station's radio. I stopped to hear more and saw one fireman give another fireman some money. He must have bet on the Dodgers.

I didn't usually look at the New York Times. There were too many ads crowding out the stories, but I loved baseball and there was a lot going on in the 1951 series. It was DiMaggio's last and Mantle's first. Mantle caught a cleat in a drain cover and wrenched his knee during the second game. I wished it were DiMaggio that got hurt. I never liked him. I liked Ted Williams and Ted Williams didn't like DiMaggio, so neither did I.

I was rooting for the Giants to win the series. All the Seneca boys around me, though, were rooting for Yankee pitcher Allie Reynolds because he was Creek Indian from Oklahoma. He went 2 and 0 and the Yankees won it in six games.

While reading about the sixth game of the World Series in the October 7th New York Times, that's where I saw the Escher prints. In particular I saw M.C. Escher's picture of the desiccated frog in the "Style" section. Of course I didn't know what 'desiccated' meant beforehand, but I did the minute I saw that picture. Immediately I wanted to show Oskee that picture.

When the lower meadow flooded from a heavy rain, small ground frogs came out from the soil near the roots of an old willow. There were always hundreds of them hopping around, looking for mates I guess. Oskee chased after them and sometimes caught one. He held it and caressed its head and studied it closely, gently feeling its profile, the bulge in its eyes, the hinged legs, like a blind man would. He seemed to etch the mottle of its coloring in his mind before setting it free. Then he would chase after another and do the same with the next one he caught.

He didn't catch more than two or three after any given rain. Oskee wasn't very coordinated, but he loved to sketch pictures. He had an extraordinary gift. He was as gifted at sketching as Nick was at woodcarving. Most of Oskee's sketches depicted frogs.

"That's a good frog," said Haksot looking at one of Oskee's pictures. "Looks good enough to eat."

Oskee didn't laugh at Haksot's jokes. He had been born with fetal alcohol syndrome and was severely retarded, plus he had a cleft pallet and a deformed nose. The sounds he made were usually unintelligible. Then when he was five years old, he caught scarlet fever. Apparently, the scarlet fever made him deaf, but because of the retardation the deafness wasn't discovered until he was seven.

The One Knife family took it all in stride. Hardships and misfortunes such as this were much too common on the reservation. Every family suffered in some way. The people weren't fatalistic or even resigned; it was more that they had backbones. They stood up to all of it.

Sometimes Haksot did not call his great-grandson "Oskee." Sometimes he called him Skö:ak, "Frog." Oskee responded with a smile to this regardless of his deafness. We all agreed he had a basic ability to read lips, since he could hear and even speak for the first five years of his life. It was only after he stopped responding when his name was called that his deafness was discovered. During the year following, the family concocted a kind of country homespun sign language. Communication with Oskee was not impossible.

One day watching him caress a ground frog after a rainstorm, I asked Gramma: "What's the word for 'love' in Onodowaga?"

"In our language there is no *one* word for 'love.' It is many words. It depends on you, your relationship to things. We don't understand how that English word 'love' can have so much power wrapped up in one little word, only to get thrown around like an old toy.

"That's another thing, we don't treat relationships like they do in Reader's Digest. The people or the lands we love are the people or the land we will *die for*. Who would I give my life for? That's *who* I love. What cause would I die for? That's *what* I love. Would I give my life so the people can live? Would I die if it meant the land would survive? It's about relationships; I love what my life is worth…"

"But what about Oskee? He loves everybody and everything, but… he wouldn't die for frogs, would he?" I had to ask.

"He already has," Gramma said. "Oskee is a pure soul. He's not a person the way we are."

"But…"

"Think about it. Where does he get his kindness? He never questions. He never objects to his life. He doesn't know how; he wouldn't know why! He tries in his way to help any animal, any person in trouble without a second thought… even the kids at school who call him 'Snot.' Creating turned off his hearing, not his feelings. The only thing Oskee feels is kindness. The way he helps others is by being kind. We didn't teach him to be kind. He just *is* kind.

"Yes, when he gets older we will somehow have to teach him about danger… from people, not from animals. The purity about him… animals see that. How do the animals know? It's like that story of Daniel in the Lion's Den. They just know. Where does that come from?"

"From God?"

"Yes, Good Mind, the God in our hearts. Oskee is not separate from the Good Mind. None of us are separate from Good Mind, really; we just think we are. Where does he get his kindness? From within his own heart. Oskee and kindness are the same thing."

Oskee was fascinated by *all* of the Escher pictures the Times reproduced and reviewed. He was drawn into them; he could not put them down. He followed the mobius staircases with his fingers. He held the "intertwined, arabesque mosaic" (the Times' description) of the dark birds and white birds up close to his face and looked at them cross-eyed as though trying to insert dimension. He tried to sketch his own hand sketching his own hand just as Escher did. His eyes were full of awe.

"Hand drawing hand drawing hand," he was maybe trying to sign, his eight-year-old fingers garbling the effort.

Then the sketch of the desiccated frog caught his breath. His eyes filled with tears. He stroked the picture, his whole hand blessed the image. Oskee was both sad and spellbound.

I looked at Oskee and I looked at the picture in the Times and realized Escher's desiccated frog touched Oskee in a way I doubt I will ever understand. At the same time I saw that skeletal starkness as a wretched emblem of reservation life.

"Skö:ak," I said, though I knew he couldn't hear. "Grandfather."

He nodded his head. Maybe he read my lips.

October was my favorite month in any year, but October 1951 was special. The forests, as usual, were at the top of their beauty. They coated the hills where I lived with scarlet and amber and lavender. Tawny bushes and lime colored vines in the valleys bathed in balmy Indian summer days. The harvest moon clothed the nights with a rusty glow. Okay, I admit, October's mighty beauty had me trying to write poetry.

What made October 1951 special for me? Father Justus got canned, fired, drummed out of the Jerome Indian School. There were a lot of rumors as to why and the word "abusive" came up in all of them. As soon as I heard the word, I dictionaried it.

"Extremely offensive and insulting. Violent and cruel. Unjust and illegal." Yep, that was Father Justus.

New York State took over total control of the school from the diocese, booted out all the administrators, took down the crosses, turned the chapel into an auditorium, hired new teachers, and basically cleaned house. All religious activity was sent across the street to the Old Quaker House, which is where my father had been holding court anyway.

When I heard the news from Gramma on Saturday October 6th, I celebrated by wandering Little Ghost Creek looking for a glen filled with Sweetgum and Musclewood trees. When I found what I was looking for, I fell backwards into a pile of Sweetgum leaves and rinsed in the delicious licorice-honey aroma that splashed up around me. I squiggled and squirmed and worked that entire spicy aroma into my clothes.

Following my Sweetgum bath, I nestled in the concave trunk of a tendon-smooth Musclewood tree and blushed in the nurturing of those crimson colored, nipple-textured leaves and that womb-like navel hollow. I spent October 6th, 1951, a harvest moon day, joyously celebrating that Father Justus, my uncle, who so wrongly branded me a coward, was now assigned, according to the newspaper account, as a chaplain at a prison in Auburn, NY.

Gramma Minnie kept her job at the school. Nobody dared fire her. After that Oskee stayed overnight at the school often since Nick was living fulltime with his mother. It wasn't easy walking Oskee back and forth to the farmhouse at night and in the early morning without Nick's help.

Some of the permanent residents among the orphan boys and maybe all of the orphan girls were known to cry themselves to sleep at night. Oskee didn't. I don't know how he knew, but if a younger child was aching and lonely, Oskee comforted, he soothed, and he held their hands and caressed their faces.

When Jimmy John cried out in his nightmares, Oskee even went to his side and soothed him. Jimmy didn't awaken, didn't know Oskee had calmed him. In daylight Jimmy was one of the mean kids, one of the ones who called Oskee 'Snot' because of Oskee's deformed and constantly mucous-dripping nose.

No one could fathom how he knew of the others' suffering, since he was so deaf, but somehow he knew...

Oskee made sounds even though he couldn't hear them. When he was comforting others, "Nikitsa, Nikitsa..." was the sound he made. Gramma said it meant, "Be calm, be peaceful." She said it was Good Mind talking through Oskee.

There was another story that caught my eye in that New York Times of October 7, 1951. It was a story about something I could not fathom. It was the story that I cut out and saved in my treasure box. It was about a holy man in the country of India who, it said, set himself on fire.

I asked my father to explain. He muttered something about "spontaneous combustion," but said he thought that only happened in haystacks.

I asked my sixth grade teacher, Mrs. Bateson, and she said: "It can't be true. No one can do that. It must be some magic trick. That Krishna figure, that's a false god, tool of the devil."

Mrs. Bateson had been my third grade teacher, only then she had been Miss Firth. Getting married moved her up several grades. I didn't like her much when I was in third grade and it looked like things weren't going to get better in sixth grade. She was the one who had us recite the Pledge of Allegiance and the Lord's Prayer morning and noon, and sing one of the three patriotic anthems twice a day. She was the teacher who used *My Weekly Reader* as proof that we were in imminent danger of being invaded by Russians. During one of her lectures one Friday afternoon early in the school year, I sat at my desk by the windows in the left rear corner in the room and fantasized shooting and picking off Russian paratroopers one-by-one as they floated down out of the skies over Bethlehem.

Mrs. Bateson kept pushing Eisenhower for President, too. She even handed out "I Like Ike" buttons. I knew my father liked Stevenson. I took one of the buttons but didn't wear it.

For all that, it was because Mrs. Bateson was a Baptist that I didn't trust her explanation of the Holy Man's feat. Instead, I turned to Gramma Minnie that next weekend after the World Series.

"Gramma! Look to this." I waved the Times story at her to get her attention. Then I deliberately read it aloud. To tell the truth, I had never seen Gramma read anything. I assumed she could; I mean, I figured she had to read recipes and labels in the Jerome kitchen where she worked. But I didn't want to embarrass her if she couldn't read, so I slowly sounded out the words I wasn't used to:

"A Hindu Holy Man burned himself to death in a small North Indian village on a day associated with the Hindu God, *Krishna*. He ignited without apparent cause through some spiritual feat using his body as fuel, and burned to death calmly with no *distinguishable* pain or anguish. The flames that rose out of the man's *abdomen* took deep structure and burned with no greenish or bluish terminal hue usual when bodies burn. The bones were reduced to ashes. His frame burned dark and dry, not the typical pale and wet. *Subcutaneous* (I stumbled over that word) skin did not surface, the internal organs burned to ashes, and fatty acids reduced in *glycerol* form. (Stumbled over that one too.) A six-hour candle-like flame consumed the man's body and produced a pleasant aroma instead of the bad odor of normal human body burns. The straw mattress on which he sat and the clothes he wore burned only with the body and during the course of hours. Said to be 110 years old, the Holy Man had been sitting in *meditation* for thirteen years. During that time no one observed him eat or drink."

"How can that be, Gramma? How could someone do that?"

Gramma took the paper out of my hands and looked at it briefly, then set it down.

"If a fire were burning in front of you, Hunter, would you know what it is?"

"Yeah, Gram... It's... a fire."

"Is that so, Hunter?" she asked quizzically, smiling.

"Yes, Gramma..."

"And, Hunter, would you know the reason for it burning?"

"It burns because I give it fuel, Gramma..."

"Is that so, Hunter?" Gramma Minnie's repetitive "Is that so, Hunter" was very deliberate, though I wasn't sure why. She continued: "And, Hunter, would you know if it were necessary to be put out?"

"Yeah, Gramma, if the fire becomes too hot or too big, or if I had to leave it alone, then I would put it out." I was getting impatient. I wanted to know how this guy could set himself on fire.

She smiled. "And on the fire being put out, Hunter, would you know where the fire went -- east, south, west, north?"

"That's, ummh, impossible, Gramma. Without fuel it dies."

"Is that so…?"

I looked at her in bewilderment.

"If it's out, how could it go somewhere else, Gramma?"

"Wholeness has a temperature," she replied.

"What do you mean?" I was fully confused.

She led me over to the potbelly stove where herbs were simmering in a closed pot on the iron lid. She held out her hands.

"Feel the warmth?"

Following her nod, I did the same. I nodded.

"It all starts with heat. Heat, the temperature, gives birth to the light. There's no light without heat, and yet they are not separate."

I put my hands down, nodded again, pretending to understand.

Gramma smiled. "Warmth and light, a hearth fire, is a gift to human beings from Creating. We are the only creatures on Mother Earth who can control Fire. That's what makes us unique among all the living beings. It is a very great responsibility that Creating bestowed, because She has a twin brother. His name is Destroying. We humans have a responsibility to use Fire creatively, not destructively. We see both Creating and Destroying in Fire. Look at the newspaper again. What else happened that day?"

She points out a story on the front page. The United States had blown up an island in the South Pacific with a hydrogen bomb. Yep, Gramma knew how to read…

"I don't get it."

"Everything is connected in Spirit. The heat in a bomb is the heat that took the Holy Man's body away is the heat in the fire in the stove. Heat is whole. Light comes alive in our eyes. Heat is felt everywhere, all the time. It just has different temperatures. Sometimes, it's even freezing. It's still heat, just degraded heat. That Holy Man; he did that with his being-mind, his will-to-exist mind."

"Wha'dya mean?"

"The story says he had been meditating for thirteen years without eating. How did he keep the fire inside going? He didn't set himself on fire. He *was*, maybe still is, the heat, the temperature, the wholeness that is everywhere."

She turned back to the stove where she had been cooking before I interrupted her. The grease in the big fry pan was just on the verge of smoking.

"Stand back," she said. "This is heat of a different texture."

From a cutting board she pushed raw scallops of squash, cut-from-the-cob corn, shredded pork, green beans, and a bunch of different greens into the fry pan. When the corn and squash hit the hot lard in the cast-iron pan, the grease popped and splashed. Some drops spattered on the old pewter mugs that sat on the stove shelf above the skillet. She put them there deliberately, she once told me, "because the grease keeps them from corroding."

"Heat is the most transformational power in the universe. Heat brings out textures, aromas, colors, flavors, sounds. We can touch heat. Songs make us feel warm, and on the other side, the warm glow we feel inside when we like someone makes us sing songs."

Just then Haksot walked through the door from the porch. He must have smelled the food.

"Speaking of songs," Haksot said, "After supper, Hunter, I need you to build a fire for the burning water lodge. I think we might just take you in there for a door or two, see how you do. You manage to make relationships with the Stone People, we'll take you to the Great Stone at the end of next month."

Haksot sat down at the table and moved the bandanna on his neck around so that it served as a bib.

"I wish Nick was here," he muttered.

Norma came in from the parlor, Oskee tagging after. Norma picked up plates and utensils from a sideboard, set them on the table, then sat down.

I glanced at her. I knew by this time that she was pregnant; it glowed on her skin color and showed in her mood. She was so pretty. I wanted to sing songs about her.

Finally, October 1951, when I was three-quarters the way through my twelfth walk around the sun, Haksot took me into the first burning water lodge I was ever in. The folks in the lodge with me were Haksot and two other old men who were friends of Haksot and I think were False Face Doctors.

They told me to sit opposite the door. Once we were all settled, Haksot asked for one hot stone to be brought in. He put cedar on it, said some words in Onodowaga, and then sat back.

"Grandson," he began. He had never called me that before. "Tell us your Dreaming, you know the one. Tell us exactly. Don't add to it. Don't subtract from it."

I did as I was told the best that I could do. When I finished, everyone said "Unnhh!" It meant they had listened and heard.

"Kaskwa:a!" Haksot barked. "Stones!"

A young nephew of one of the old men brought in the rest of the stones, fifteen more, one by one on a hayfork. The stones were glowing red-hot.

When the stones were all in, the flap over the entrance came down. It was pitch dark except for the glowing stones which didn't really illuminate anything but themselves. Haksot started praying in his language.

True to the Longhouse tradition, he prayed from beginning to end with gratitude. That night I learned, Longhouse Way, to express gratitude for things that hadn't yet occurred.

He always began with:

"Hotyε:no'kta?oh. Creating, Nyah Weh S'geno, Thank You for Being.

"Your messenger, the Spirit here standing in the sacred center, Oshata?ke':a?, Dew Eagle, Nyah Weh S'geno, Thank You for Being.

"Old men taught me this way, and if I make a mistake, thank you for you turn it into good. Thank you for pitying me."

He expressed "gratitude for health and help for everyone in the lodge... way out into life ahead until you call us again to this place that we may renew again with tears our gratitude." He was always grateful for protection... against any harm over which we have no control.

In English he said, "Thank you for guiding this boy; the Dreaming he had, his vision of Spirit Trail Woman, what it means for him, what it means for us, how to help, how to honor, what to do, what you need from us, our sacrifice. Thank you for instructing us.

"Thank you for you the power to carry well your thoughts and guidance. Thank you for continued peace in One Mind that we do this properly."

After the opening prayer, the other old men sang a song. The only word I recognized was "Oshatakea," "Dew Eagle," so I figured they were honoring the spirit Haksot said was standing in the center on the stones.

Haksot put water on the stones and it got really hot, but at the same time comforting. By the time the song was finished, I had taken to the world of the burning water lodge with no internal conflict. I felt at home.

Haksot opened and closed the door three times, and with each pitch-dark round the warm got more intense and the songs took longer. Behind the songs Haksot prayed earnestly, entirely in his language.

Before the fourth door closed, he spoke in English to all of us. Later I was told he interpreted what Spirit, Dew Eagle, said to him:

"To live and move in the Dreaming is hard work. Takes discipline. In the Dreaming, time is different, places are strange; we're invisible. To live and move there we must call upon Power to pick us up; to do otherwise is foolish. Once picked up by Power, our lives are *owed* in service to the People and the Earth and with gratitude. If it is used otherwise, someone's life, a relative, will be taken. So most of us only go there, we don't stay there, we don't ask to be picked up."

He paused as though puzzled, yet his voice sounded relieved.

"In your Dreaming you saw Spirit Trail Woman, Fat Face. She pulled you from the quicksand; she picked you up. She sent you back to start over."

He paused again, as though listening.

"Spirit said 'invisible.' It means 'no identity.' You are not Indian; you are not... anyone. My job, our job, is to help you sustain that. Have no identity; you connect to the Dreaming of the first dawn. You are young in age, old in mind. Even so, the matter will be difficult."

Haksot closed the door. There was no glow from the stones; we were in consuming darkness, no projections, no reflections. The False Face doctors slapped their turtle rattles on the ground. They used the Earth as a drum, the rattles as a beater.

It got very hot, very hot. Dizzy, I fell over. There was singing, many voices, from every direction, and then I saw a Jo?kä:oh, a Little Person, who looked like the Friend who came to me when I was tied to the porch. He was hopping up and down like a frog, pointing at the Earth and silently screaming at me.

# 12
# *THE WHITE HOTEL*

Twenty-eight miles south of Bethlehem on US 20 in a basin alongside Lake Erie sat the resort town of Crystal Springs. My father grew up there, his grandfather once owned a bar there, and my Uncle Joe and Aunt Dorothy, before their divorce, owned and operated *JoeDot's* hardware, furniture and antique store there.

Many of its houses were Victorians with three floors and wrap-around porches. Not Uncle Joe's. He built a newfangled home, all red brick and picture windows with a covered thing they called a 'lanai' off the kitchen in back. In the basement was a recreation room with a pinball machine and a bumper pool table. My buck-toothed cousin Wendell, six years older than me, was devilishly good at pool. I never won a single game from him; however, Wendell did teach me the fundamentals like bank-and-kiss shots and 'putting English on the ball.'

I loved visiting there. Uncle Joe and Aunt Dorothy were among the first people I knew to own a television. I saw my first Rose Bowl game – Michigan destroyed California forty-nine to nuthin' - on their TV.

Back in June 1948, Uncle Joe bought a purple Buick-Roadmaster convertible with the famous Dynaflow transmission, the first torque-converter automatic transmission on an American-built car. I remember because it was the year Henry Ford died. Father had called Ford a fascist and vowed he would never own a Ford-built car. Right after Uncle Joe bought the Roadmaster, he drove it directly to our house. I thought Father would be pleased because it wasn't a Ford, but instead it seemed to make my father jealous, and Uncle Joe particularly seemed to savor his older brother's envy.

"Poverty is a virtue" was a constant theme of my father's sermons, and his reasoning for never giving me spending money. Still, I could tell when Father was jealous.

"Is Uncle Joe rich?" I asked my father after my uncle drove away.

"Why do you ask?" Father grumbled. He was in a bad mood; we only drove a Chevy.

"'Cause if he's rich, does that mean he's gonna go to hell?"

"He's not that rich," Father said.

"'Cause if he isn't rich, but he is a crook, he's going to hell anyway... and if he is rich but he isn't a crook... "

"Just drop it, will you? Where do you come up with these ideas?"

"I read the Bible, remember? It's easier for a camel to pass through the eye of a needle than it is for a rich man to get into heaven."

"He's lucky, that's all. He married into money. Their store was always in *her* family."

*My father married into money too, why aren't we lucky?* I thought and considered asking, but figured it would get me a swat across the back of my head.

*Damn*, I thought. (I was trying to read Pudd'nhead Wilson at the time and Puddn'head said, "damn" a lot.) *If Uncle's Joe's going to hell, well maybe I am too 'cause my problem was*

*Commandment #10: Thou Shalt Not Covet! I coveted a Buick Roadmaster. I coveted a television set. I coveted cousin Wendell's pool table. I took no comfort in the fact that Commandment #10 had a 'neighbor' clause in it. Wendell technically wasn't my neighbor, however... he was a blood relative. How could I not be sinning?*

Once, somewhere in the course of those years spent with Gramma Minnie, I asked her if she ever 'coveted.' I hoped she would say "yes," and then I wouldn't feel so guilty. Instead, her answer skipped twenty steps ahead of my question:

"For three hundred years we've been watching the Clay People mistranslate our language. We figure they did the same thing with the words in the Bible. We don't have 'shalt nots.' We have suggestions: 'Do it this way and you won't suffer consequences.' Those commandments – we think a better word is 'instructions.' 'Covet' and 'sin' - we have no words for those concepts. In the old days we shared everything – a lot of us still do, it's natural law. God's instruction about coveting?... hmm... we believe the way to serve God is to help people. Coveting is not helping."

A month after he bought the Roadmaster, Uncle Joe divorced Aunt Dorothy and moved to South Carolina. Apparently he took quite a lot of money and someone I overheard my father call "the town slut" with him.

For the next three years, my father and I went to Crystal Springs once a month to visit the graves of my father's parents. On Memorial Day we'd stop and pick wildflowers from a field along the way. It was my job to place them. That was weird, I thought. Since my father's parent's died before I was born, my only memory of them was flowers my father was too cheap to buy lying on top of their names on a rectangular gravestone sinking in the grass.

That graveyard was across a gully from the White Hotel, the 100-year-old centerpiece of Crystal Springs. I always wondered what it was like inside; it was so grand, so elegant, so impressive. There were always Cadillac Devilles and Packard Broughams and Lincoln Cosmopolitans in the parking lot whenever we drove by.

We never stopped. I never went inside, never strolled up the tree-lined slate sidewalk, touched the porticos, or opened the wide oak front door. I never considered I might one day eat in the restaurant or stand at the entrance to the Grand Ballroom.

I never did any of that until my mother and my grandfather (the one I hadn't met – the one who sent me ten dollars every Christmas) traveled to Western NY in November 1951 and stayed for several nights at the White Hotel. They came on the weekend I was supposed to go with Gramma and Haksot to the Great Stone at the north end of Canandaigua Lake.

A year earlier, Mother had suffered her terrible accident that I still felt was my fault. After that accident, I spent weeks in mute isolation in the Indian School orphanage being bullied and called a coward by Father Justus. My ten-year-old mind accepted that God was punishing me for hurting my mother. Every time I saw my mother -- or even got a letter from her -- I felt terrible sickening guilt over causing her disfigurement. And I had it in the back of my mind that Gramma Minnie had said that my mother would be "coming for me."

Father told me Mother wanted to see me, but he also made it sound like a summons from the Grandfather. Father didn't ask me if I wanted to see her. If he had asked, I would've said "no," and especially not on that weekend.

But my father didn't ask how I felt. So after chores on Saturday, November 8, I put on my Sunday suit, polished my shoes, clipped on a bowtie and rode with Father to Crystal Springs and the White Hotel.

As we were ascending the steep two-mile long hairpin-turn hill that took us south out of Bethlehem and onto the state route that gradually descended through the next twenty miles into Crystal Springs, I asked, "Father? What does 'raped' mean?"

Father was in the middle of downshifting from third to second our brand new blue and white Fleetline Chevrolet. It always took second gear to pull that hairpin hill into the heights above the town.

At the sound of the word "raped" Father literally missed the clutch and crunched second gear.

Father muttered something Irish under his breath, then said, "Where did you hear that word?"

"At Gramma Minnie's... Norma said it. She was talking about being pregnant and then she said she had been raped. What's raped?"

"Did she say anything else?"

"No."

"Did she say she was drunk when it happened?"

"Yeah. I heard Gramma ask her if she was pregnant one morning when Norma was throwing up, and then Norma told her and Gramma told Haksot. Haksot was real gruff with her when she said being pregnant was not her fault because she was raped, and then Haksot said it *was* her fault 'cause she was drunk. So, I guess... sorta. But, what's 'raped' mean?"

"Son..." Father started to say. He hardly ever called me 'son,' except when he was about to give me a 'run-around.' "How old are you?"

*Holy Shit,* I thought. (I was in sixth grade and learned 'holy shit' from the Italian kids.) *He knows how old I am. He's really fishing for an answer. Raped must be some kinda serious.*

"I'm eleven. I looked 'rape' up in the dictionary. It said forced 'sexual intercourse' by a man on another person without their consent and against their will, especially by violence.' Then it had a sentence about the timber industry raping the land. I don't understand how that and being pregnant go together. What's 'sexual intercourse'? Is that how they cut down trees?"

"Son…." Father began again. "There's some things… a boy your age just shouldn't worry about… and this is one of them."

"But…"

"I can't explain it. It's adult stuff. Anyway, child psychology is not my forté."

"What's a 'forté'?"

"Just forget it, okay?"

By this point, Father was so flustered he had to drop another gear into first. At least he didn't crunch that gear.

We drove the rest of the way to Crystal Springs in silence. When Father finally stopped in front of the White Hotel, he reached over and put his hand on my shoulder.

"Now listen to me. If they ask where you were while I was in Rochester, tell them you were in camp the *whole time.* Will you do that? Say nothing about spending time on the reservation. You were in camp the whole time, understand?"

I nodded a bewildered "yes."

"And whatever you do — what *ever* you do — don't ask your mother what 'rape' means, or even mention Norma or Mavis. Got it? Nothing. Zip your lip. No 'rape.'"

I nodded again but started to protest. Father cut me off: "Your mother wants custody of you. Right now you live with me because she spent time in a mental hospital after the accident."

He paused; maybe to let that fact sink in.

"If she knew about the amount of time you spend at Minnie's, your grandfather -- he's a Judge you know -- he would make a legal case that I'm a bad father."

"Why?"

"Because... because they're Indians."

"But what...?"

"He would say they're pagans, and in the eyes of the law that's bad. You'll end up living with your mother in Pennsylvania and you'll never see Gramma Minnie again. So, whatever else you talk about and whatever else you say to them, do *not* talk about the time you spend on the reservation. Don't talk about what you do there. Don't talk about your dream. Okay?"

Again I nodded "yes," but the claws of a bad feeling had hold of me.

"Okay. I'll be back to pick you up out front here at 4 o'clock. Don't be late."

I nodded "yes" yet again and opened the door. The Chevy still had that new car smell and the light breeze in the fifty-degree November air picked it up and made me smile. I was proud we had a new car.

"Oh, another thing... if they ask about the paperwork, it's at the office of the cemetery. Paperwork, office, cemetery... can you remember that... if they ask...?

Baffled, I nodded "yes" for the fourth time -- and then all alone and feeling very small and nervous, and wishing I was in Canandaigua, I walked up the tree-lined slate sidewalk of the White Hotel.

# 13
## *STIEFKIND ~ ~ STEPCHILD*

I heard it said the restored twice and white-washed umpteen times White Hotel was built to serve the New Yorkers who couldn't afford the resorts at Chautauqua.

The brass on the front doors gleamed. The reception desk was carved from one oak tree trunk cut down when the hotel was built. The bar served French brandy from squat bottles wrapped in wicker, and whiskey from white oak casks, which according to a plaque on the wall were staved in winter, whatever that meant.

"Miss Koenig is in room six on the second floor. You can take the stairs or the elevator," the waxen lady behind the oak desk smiled.

Before that moment I had never been in an elevator. The only elevators in Bethlehem were in the hospital, and children weren't allowed in the hospital unless they were sick. So of course I was thrilled to take the elevator, even though I had no idea how it worked.

The White Hotel had an old, clanking, metal-gate elevator and a brass door that slid closed so fast it knocked me sideways. Once inside I didn't know what to do. There was a brass plate with two black buttons that had no markings. I felt trapped. I got a little scared and pushed the bottom black button. An annoying and loud "wrong!" buzz sound racketed. The old box elevator actually shuddered. I broke into a sweat.

The brass door and the gate were heavy, but I got them open again, though the heavy sliding door knocked my hat off my head. I escaped the elevator cage and, hat in hand, climbed the wide, multi-color, carpeted stairs. The hard soles of my Sunday shoes made a slipping sound; the carpet must have been an inch thick. The light fixtures in alcoves on the walls were polished old brass gaslights, refitted as electric. It was all so elegant, so… self-assured.

Me? I felt small and alone.

When I got to the landing I stopped and looked out the big arch window. Across the parking lot and a gully I could see headstones. Even at that distance they looked familiar, but it was the old, grey stonewall that circled and set it apart from the rest of the area that made me realize it was the Protestant cemetery where the German side of my family were buried.

I stood and looked out that window what seemed like an hour but was probably a minute. Then I trudged up the second set of wide stairs from the landing to the second floor hallway.

I stopped again at the top of the stairs that tee'd into the middle of a hallway. Which way was Room Six – left or right?

"Feel it," that's what Gramma Minnie would say. "Don't know which way to go, don't think it -- feel it. In fact it's best not to say what you're thinking. There's already enough confusion on this planet. Thinking is, after all, just fixin' to get ready to plan to do something."

Feeling was tough for me. Father and Mother had taught me to ask questions. They encouraged me to think. Before my days with Haksot and Gramma Minnie, the only feelings I ever had were shame and guilt. I was never taught to feel, just feel – like warmth and joy - until I spent time on the reservation.

But I stood in that hallway thinking, planning what I would say to a person, my mother, who only ever encouraged the parts of me that were hers and otherwise barely tolerated the rest of me.

I was nervous, uncertain, scared even. Scared of the guilt I felt. I hadn't seen Mother in almost a year, and I didn't really want to see her now. Plus, I had to pee. I reached in to loosen my underwear and adjust myself before I tightened down on the urge to pee.

A door opened. Mother stepped halfway out, looked left, then right, and then saw me. Did she feel I was in the hallway? Did she know I had to pee, or that I resented even being there?

Her timing, this time, was only near-perfect. She was so good at catching me doing something of which she disapproved. Thank God this time I got my hands out of my pants before she saw me.

She smiled. "Hunter, there you are. Come…"

I wiggle-walked, hat in hand, down the inch-thick red and gold rug.

She reached out and touched my cheek. "Liebchen… it's good to see you. It's been too long."

"I have to pee," is the first thing I said to her.

The smile vanished. She held the door open and nodded me in.

*Oops, I should have said 'tinkle.' Mother regards 'piss, pee, whiz' as crude. Oh well, she will just have to get used to me the way I am now.*

I carefully closed the door of her bathroom. I knew that Mother didn't like the sound of pissing. When I was little, she toilet-trained me to sit down to pee because I made less noise that way. It upset her to hear the stream hit the water in the bowl. Maybe there was a connection between her dressing me in girl's clothes for the first two years of my life and training me to sit even when 'tinkling.'

It was an old toilet and the water was really high in it, but I refused to sit to piss just to please her. I aimed at the section of white porcelain that was above the water line, but I missed and instead pissed on the edge of the bowl. A lot of the yellow spray went on the little white six-sided tiles on the floor and some even splattered on my pant leg.

I pushed Fred to the right (I named my wiener "Fred" when I was in fourth grade after I heard some other kid call his wiener "Dick") and got the stream all in the bowl, but now I was making noise. I flushed to cover the noise I was making, but the flush finished before I did. As the water refilled, I had more porcelain to hit, so I wasn't making noise, but the water in the bowl was now turning yellow! Mother also did not like yellow water.

*Oh well, she'll just have to get used to me the way I am now.*

I buttoned up my fly and flushed a second time; oh Christ... I should have grabbed some toilet paper and cleaned up the edge of the bowl and the floor before I flushed.

*Jesus, that was dumb, now there's gonna be folded-up pieces of toilet paper floating in the water. She won't like that either. Holy Cow, I don't want to flush it a third time. Oh well, she'll just have to get used to...*

"Don't forget to wash you hands and face," she called from the other side of the door. "We're going to dinner soon."

I turned on the water in the sink and ran it loud to cover the sound of my third flushing of the toilet. When I stuck my hands under the faucet, the force of the water was so strong that it splashed all over my suit coat and my pants.

*Christ, now it looks like I pissed my pants.*

"Jesus, Joseph and Mary," I muttered, remembering the Irish in me. "I can't goddamn win."

"What did you say?"

*Holy shit, is she standing on the other side of the door listening to my every move?*

Suddenly the door opened. "Did you swear? Does your father know you swear? Where did you learn to do that?"

There was a look of disgust in Mother's eyes that I had never seen before. I felt like a puppy that crapped on the floor and was about to have his nose rubbed in it.

Mother clucked her tongue, then stepped aside and allowed me to exit the bathroom. As I went by her, her arm moved and I ducked. I thought she was going to grab me by the ear and drag me out of the bathroom like my second grade teacher, Old Maid McCanty, once did. But Mother was just moving to adjust the hand towel that I obviously did not hang properly. Everything had to be just right with her.

"Swearing is crude and obnoxious. Swearing is a sign of poor toilet training. You did *not* have poor toilet training. Are you learning to swear from the Indians? I know you spend a lot of time with them. Your father can't hide that from us."

"Everybody swears," I say. "Even at church… sometimes … well, Carson Baily."

"Hah!" said Mother. "Him, I don't doubt."

"You're the only person I know who doesn't swear. I guess we all had poor toilet training, huh?" I surprised myself saying that, but my attitude, my swallowing the required apology, excited me even though it bordered on disrespect.

I figured what I said would anger her, but unexpectedly she reached out and gently touched my face. I saw a tear in her right eye.

"Stiefkind," she said. "I hardly know you." It sounded sad, not angry.

*Stiefkind? Stepchild?*

"You use to call me 'stepchild' when you were mad at me. You don't look mad. Are you...?"

"You mean angry, not mad... and I know you know that. But I'm neither." (She pronounced neither with the long I.) "I'm... upset. You've changed."

*Oh well...* "I haven't seen you in almost a year. You've changed too."

"How have I changed?" It was very direct, unlike her usual reticence.

She had color back in her skin and her natural hair had grown out. It was set different, combed over the side of her head that the bull had kicked. She had a glass eye in her left eye. That kind of unnerved me. I kept trying not to look at it but it was like I was seeing her for the first time. She took my staring with a dry smile. She didn't give me any one-eyed, return look that made me feel bad, though I wondered if she saw me as a stranger.

"Have a seat," she said, indicating a rickety looking antiquely upholstered chair. "I'll just be another minute."

Mother liked her room, I could tell. I watched her as she moved about, getting last-minute ready, caressing the ball on a bed post and doting over the fancy, flowered-glass lampshades on the antique nightstands.

"Isn't this beautiful?" She stood at a vanity table with a floral print porcelain washbasin. "It's wormwood maple."

She was putting on her pearl earrings. "This is a well-dressed room. I must remember to tip the maid," she murmured.

She adjusted her pearl necklace, and then turned to look at me. "Are you comfortable?"

*No,* I think but I don't dare say so.

"I like the rug." The 9x12 rug was thick and its deep red wool blended warmly with the dark oak floor. There were lace curtains over white oak shutters at the window, and a linen tablecloth and silver tea-set on the corner table. I walked over to the teapot and touched it. "Wow, is this real silver?"

"Isn't it grand? And how did you know to recognize that"

"You used to have silver along with your china set. You never let me eat eggs with it. You said the sulfur in the eggs would wreck it."

"We'll, I'm sure I didn't say 'wreck'." She put on a cashmere sweater with a mink stole. "I still have that silver and that china… someday when you marry… that is, if you want…"

"Yeah, sure."

"Are you eating well? Does your father cook, or does he get that Indian woman to do it for him?"

"He cooks. We have a lot of macaroni and hot dogs. Church people have us over a lot. I eat lunch at school. Breakfast is Cheerios and rye toast."

"On Wednesdays… do you eat at the orphanage before Bible class?"

"Not anymore. The state took over the Indian School and kicked all the religions out. We only go there on holidays. Father Justus got canned."

"Really? Well, that's good news… hideous man. That whole Irish side of the family…" She looks away.

"Once a month," I offer, remembering that Father said to steer clear of the reservation, "after church on Sundays we come over here and have dinner with Aunt Dorothy and Wendell. Then we go visit the cemetery… oh, and Father said to tell you that the signed papers are in the office of the cemetery… whatever that means."

Mother regarded me with what looked like narrow suspicion in her one good eye. Then she went to the door and opened it and with a nod indicated we were leaving the room.

"We're having a dinner with your grandparents. My father is a judge. He can be brusque, curt even, but he doesn't mean any harm. That's just his way. Don't be upset by it."

*Thanks for the warning,* I thought. I had never met my grandparents. There was genuine dislike between my father and the Judge. My father once told me my grandfather refused to come to my parents' wedding. I guess the problem started there.

Going out the door, I asked: "Aren't you going to tip the maid?"

"Later," she said.

# 14

## *SINGING WOMAN*

My grandfather, the Judge, was overweight, balding, white-mustached, ruddy-faced, and wheezing from asthma or some other lung disease. He looked me up and down, accepted my offered hand, but didn't smile.

"He doesn't look like us. He looks like him," he said to my mother as we sat down on plush red velvet chairs to a white tablecloth, crystal glasses, and cloth napkins in a chandeliered dining room. "You sure you want to do this?"

"Quite sure," Mother said.

*Do what*, I wondered while glancing with curiosity at my grandmother. She was tiny, frail, timid, but with more love in her eyes than I had ever seen from anyone else in my blood family. Her hands shook nervously.

I looked around the dining room. It was half-full of men in suits with vests and watch chains and women in big hats and loud broaches. Clinking sounds from silver forks mingled with pings from crystal wineglasses and cheerful giggles and hollow chatter. 'Simple with pearls,' an expression my mother often used to describe herself, didn't apply to the rest of the diners. Showy was a better word.

"Hunter, this is your grandmother," Mother said, covering her embarrassment. "She has an illness called

Parkinson's. That's what makes her shake. But her mind is totally alert. You can talk to her."

Grandmother had a sweet smile, but there was grey spittle at the corners of her mouth.

"Hello, Grandmother," I said, picking up her hand and shaking it lightly. It was tiny and fragile with brown spots and blue veins.

"Hunter. You are a fine looking boy. I'm so happy to finally meet you," she said with a weak, piper's voice.

Quick and sudden, the Judge grabbed my wrist and shook me with his hammer-hand.

"Your *real* Grandmother. Your real one, understand?"

I sat there with my left wrist in his grip and felt a cold fright drill down my spine from neck to tail.

"What do you mean?" I puppy-whimpered.

"You know exactly what I mean," he snarled as he let go of my wrist. "We know all about the… "

"Judge! You promised..."

*My gosh, she calls her own father 'Judge'.* My eyes burned hearing that.

I had counted two-dozen people in the room. As I listened to my grandfather wheeze and cough and snort phlegm into his handkerchief with a farmer-fart sound that made at least a dozen of the two-dozen look around, I wondered if he would leave any air for the rest of us to breathe.

*Jesus,* I thought. *If I had table manners like that Mother would hit _me_ with a wooden spoon.*

Salvation arrived in the form of a waiter with a covered china tureen and four bowls. The slick, mustached server dished out the soup with a silver ladle. He put a bowl in front of each of us starting with my shaking Grandmother.

Mother's right eye looked at me and then at my cloth napkin, then helped her mother with her napkin. I dutifully put my napkin on my lap.

Judge Grandfather sniffed at the soup, then took a sip.

"It isn't hot enough. Waiter! It isn't hot enough. Take it back and heat it up. And there's a draft from the furnace vent blowing on me. Could we sit at a different table?"

He abruptly stood up. The rest of us followed more slowly. With difficulty, I pushed Grandmother's wheelchair, I guess because the Judge had already bolted for another table. Mother showed me how to release the brake on the wheel.

"Now the fan is worse. This won't do at all."

He hadn't even sat down at the new table and now was scowling again. No, it was more than scowling. There was an Old Testament wrath in his forehead and peril in the veins in his neck. I figured any moment he would blow a gasket.

Back at our first table, as the waiter stood motionless like a bird-dog at point, the Judge turned and disdainfully said: "The rolls are cold now too. Would the waiter bring fresh warm ones?" He looked right at him and called him "the waiter."

I had always been embarrassed by my mother's timidity, the way she shrank back from men; the way she never spoke up for herself. That day, the way I watched my grandfather push family and servants around as if he owned us, I understood why. Mother had lived with him for the first 21 years of her life and now was living with him again.

And maybe my grandmother didn't have anything else wrong with her except that she quaked in fear of 'the Judge.'

The waiter frog-walked back to the kitchen to start the first course over. Mother's nervous habit of writing words on tables with the index finger of her right hand went into overdrive. I'd watched her do that when we were together. I'd prided myself that I could read her cursive fingernail writing even upside down. She wrote "custody" and then "ceiling fan" and then "fawn" on the tablecloth.

There's that word "custody" that Father mentioned.

The waiter returned directly with a different tureen and clean bowls and a new basket of rolls.

"I trust this is to your honor's satisfaction," the waiter plied.

"It better be," the Judge said.

I ate my soup and then ate two rolls from the basket. The rolls were delicious, all doughy and hot and sweet and there was real butter on the table, not the war-surplus white lard margarine that my father bought.

When the waiter set my dinner plate in front of me, the Judge said: "I ordered for you. Just for the halibut... haw, haw, haw!"

It was fish, a kind I never had before, and little red potatoes and asparagus. It was all right. At least the fish didn't have eyes in it the way Gramma Minnie would have cooked it. Someone picked out almost all the bones, too.

There was a white sauce that came with the fish that I really liked. My mother had the same meal I had, but she also had white wine.

"What book are you reading this month," Mother asked between bites.

I gulped and said, "Pudd'nhead Wilson."

"Damn," said the Judge. "You can read that? How old are you?" My grandfather stuffed food into his mouth and talked while he ate. He was eating pork with scalloped potatoes and sauerkraut. *I loved scalloped potatoes,* I thought. *Why didn't he get that for me? Asshole...*

Sometimes bits of the kraut spilled out of his mouth onto the table and floor. Mother would kill me if I ate like that. As for my Grandmother, well, her hand never stopped shaking, but she always got the food onto the fork and into her mouth.

"I started teaching him to read at age three," Mother countered. "He's always been years ahead of his age group."

"Did you enjoy Puddn'head?" my Grandmother was the only one really listening.

"Not really. It's not as funny as most of Twain's stuff. I like Huckleberry Finn better. I read that twice."

"Waiter!" boomed the Judge across the room to the Bud Abbott look-alike. "More rolls. The kid's eaten them all. And make sure they're warm."

"No I didn't..." I tried to protest.

My mother fidgety-nervous spelled Judge with a capital "J" with her index finger on the tablecloth next to her knife.

*She is really tense,* I thought. *Something's not right, something is on her mind.*

"Would you like to take a walk after dinner? Push Grandmother in the wheelchair?" Mother cut into her embarrassment again with just a slight flip of her hair on the caved-in side of her head.

"Okay." I mean, could I even try to say "no?"

"I thought we would visit Liesel's grave."

"Who's Liesel?"

"Your sister. You know… she was… lost in the accident."

*Holy shit!* I swore again in my thoughts. *This is a first. I had never been told her name. I didn't know she had been buried. I mean; she hadn't really been born.*

"Oh yeah, sure," I said but I thought *Holy Damn! Is she taking me to the grave so I can feel guilty all over again -- so I can give up and give in to whatever she wants?*

A Negro woman, the first Negro I had ever been that close to in my entire life, cleared the dishes away. Up to then I had only seen Negroes on television sports shows or on the streets of Buffalo.

The woman clearing our dishes fascinated me. Her skin was like dark honey. I handed her my plate, but she didn't look at me. She kept her head bowed near my grandfather, too, so I didn't see her face until she lifted her eyes and head in response to my Grandmother's frail but sincere "Thank you."

I started to say "thank you" when all of a sudden the waiter, who had brought something that looked like cake, lit a match and set it on fire.

"What the h… heck?" I blurted.

"Baked Alaska, my favorite," said the Judge. "You've probably never had this, right? Well, you're in for a treat, thanks to me. You come to live with us, you can have this all the time."

*Live with you?... That'll be a cold day in hell.*

<<< >>>

I pushed my patient Grandmother in her wheelchair one block south on US 20, then one block west on Second Avenue, and then back east on a rutted asphalt road.

Were it not for the wheelchair in which the strange frail woman with Parkinson's disease sat shaking in her heavy fur coat and long scarf (that I kept from tangling in the chair's spokes), I'd have cut between the Packards in the White Hotel's parking lot, run down into the gully and back up the opposite bank, then vaulted up onto the three-foot high stone wall that surrounded the graveyard and danced on the stone wall's top edge before jumping down onto the November brown lawn with its clutter of hundred-year-old gravestones awash with leaves from tall old elms.

When I turned off Second Avenue onto the asphalt road, I realized it was the entrance road to the same cemetery where my father's parents were buried. Evidently a baby named Liesel had also been buried there, but I never knew that from my father.

Pushing the wheelchair was really difficult on the rutted asphalt. I kept looking back to see if the Judge would step up and help, but he was talking at my mother, saying words such as "paperwork" and "court orders" and "exhume" with his hand nestled in the small of Mother's back. I made a mental note to dictionary "exhume."

The office of the cemetery was a stone building next to the entrance gate. There was a brand new blue-and-white Chevrolet Fleetline parked there. License number KV486. My heart beat faster. What was going on? My father said nothing about meeting us at the cemetery. He said he would pick me up at the hotel at 4PM.

There were only four steps into the stone building, but it took some effort to get the wheelchair up them. The Judge pulled from above; I pushed from the feet.

Inside, my father was waiting, leaning on a counter talking to a woman. There was a small stack of papers on the counter, and a black telephone. The room was cold and grey. Against the wall there was a wrought iron bench and two wooden armchairs. Mother quickly sat in one of them.

"I changed my mind," Father said upon our entering. "I realized your intention to exhume, you know, Liesel, is a ruse." He looked at Mother.

"You're not here for Liesel, you're here for Hunter."

"Are those the papers?" the Judge indicated.

Father nodded "yes."

"Then you can leave now," said the Judge. "Yes, we are here for Hunter *too*, just to talk to him, just to explain. But seriously, you haven't got a leg to stand on, so it behooves you to not make things worse. Don't make us take you to court."

"I'm not leaving and I won't let you shame him into living with you."

"Leave," the Judge snarled, "or I'll call the police."

The word "police" made my chest ache. There was suddenly "so much ugly" in the room I turned for the door, just wanted to get outside.

The Judge grabbed the collar of my Sunday-best overcoat with his tight fist, yanked me back, and shoved me toward the iron bench.

"Sit down, young man. It's time you heard the truth about your father and that woman you call 'Gram-maw Minnie'."

He leveled a menacing sneer at my father, but when he looked back at me the sneer was gone and for the first time I saw his smile.

"When I'm done with your father, you *will* be living with us."

He pushed me into the bench with a thud and my head bounced on the back rail. I got dizzy, real dizzy, felt like I had to throw up, and then…

*Not only did I hear her, but I saw her. She floated cardinal-right. She wore a cloak of white light. I could not see the features of her face; the light was brightest there. Between us was a misty veil.*

*"Find the way," she sang. "You're a water person, a way-finder. Find the way."*

"Water! He's fainted. Get some water and a cloth!" A man's voice… then a different man's voice: "Lay him on the floor. Lift his feet."

There was a thumping sound. I felt fear; like ice in my blood. I was falling. Then an explosion of heat, Cheshire-heat, throughout my head.

"Dammit!" Both male voices said that.

Singing Woman and the Cheshire-heat silently disappeared, replaced by fluttering, something fluttering; pages from a dream fluttering in the wind in my mind.

*I am David. I stand before Saul. I hold Goliath's head by his hair. Blood drips onto the floor from Goliath's neck. Saul looks at Goliath, looks at his hands and turns his back to me.*

*A woman blessed by the ways of the Virgin Mother soothes me with a red snake. The red snake is wet and surrounds my head.*

"Vocatus atque non vocatus Deus aderit." Someone was speaking Latin? I recognized it; Father Justus babbled Latin all the time. God; it was something about the voice of God.

"Is he speaking in tongues? Who is this kid?" Saul -- that was Saul asking, his voice distant behind me.

The snake dripped water into my eyes and unfolded into a wet red wash over my forehead.

My eyelids flickered. Light seeped in.

I opened my eyes and saw three faces: one of Confusion, one of Despair and one of Anger.

Behind me, out of sight, a royal voice was talking, probably, into the old black phone on the counter.

"Concussion, yes, I'm sure of it. He fell, hit his head hard…."

"You dropped him!" That was my father's voice. It came out of the Face of Anger.

"And he's labile… what do you mean, you don't know? It means emotionally unstable… you may have to sedate him. Yes, I know that's for you to determine, but I'm telling you he's unstable, a dreamer, an idiot."

"Judge!" That was the Face of Despair, my mother, no longer a Virgin Mother. "He's not an idiot! He's gifted."

Mother took the red washcloth from my forehead, dabbed at the tears in her eyes, and then handed the cloth to the Face of Confusion, a woman holding a bowl. She must work here. I remembered now where I was; a grey cold room in a stone house. The woman hovering over me with the bowl was the woman behind the counter when I walked in.

My father stepped back with his hands on his head, shaking with anger. Next to him, a frail old woman in a wheelchair was weeping into her lace handkerchief.

"You want custody and then you call him an idiot. Are you sick?"

"I meant 'idiot' in the legal sense. He was speaking in tongue," Saul's voice snarled. "I don't know if I want this kid around, not if he's mentally unbalanced. But you, George, you better put a sock in it. You have no call to be righteous."

"He was speaking Latin." My mother's voice cracked with anguish. "It means 'Called or not called, the gods will come.' I taught him that, years ago. I can't believe… "

The Judge's dark voice bullied, "That's even worse. He's delusional."

The Face of Confusion handed Mother the rinsed and renewed red washcloth. Mother tried to put it back on my forehead, but I didn't want it and shook my head "no."

That's when I felt the sticky wetness in the hair on the back of my head. Mother noticed it too, and her face of despair returned.

"Ah! He's bleeding," she cried. "Tell them he's bleeding!"

Judge Grandfather suddenly loomed into view.

"Too late, I hung up." He wiped his hands with white linen from his suit pocket. "Put the washcloth under his head. He'll be all right."

# 15
## *SOMEONE HAS DIED, SOMEONE IS BORN*

I sit at the feet of Franklin Delano Roosevelt. He soothes me. I feel safe and secure with him, even though there are flames all around us. At first I don't notice the fire. I only notice Franklin Delano Roosevelt. At first the heat doesn't matter. At first I feel safe and soothed, but then the flames get really hot.

I suck at my mouth but there is no spit; my mouth is dry. I pop it open; make a sucking sound, then another sound, like a groan. I groan because there's something in my mouth, some tube, some hook like the dentist uses, and some thing holding down my tongue. I shake my head from side to side but then the thing on my tongue gags me, and the fire and the heat inside my head will not go away.

The heat turns dark red. I smack my lips, they make a sound, a dry cracking sound -- or is that sound from the metal hook, the metallic, flinty, thistle-tasting hook?

Franklin Delano Roosevelt reaches out and touches my forehead.

"He's burning up. Get the nurse, this fever is too high," he says.

"Mickey sees the USA," I try to tell him, but my lips smack and the thing in my throat hurts me.

"What?" Franklin asks.

"Mickey sees the USA," I say again, hopelessly.

"I think he said…" That was a woman's voice. "It's odd, but it sounded to me he was saying the name of a book he read when he was five years old. 'Mickey Sees the USA.' He loved that book. He read it over and over."

*She must be my mother. How would she know that otherwise?*

"That's ridiculous. He's delirious… that or demented." That was an old man's voice.

Franklin Delano Roosevelt's hand is still on my forehead.

"Shut up, you dolt, and get a nurse. This fever is dangerous." Franklin sounds like my father.

The red heat turns dark purple, like the blood in the haunch of a stag I helped Haksot butcher. My eyelids are so heavy. I only see the dark fur on the haunch. The fur is tipped with white hair.

*Then…… Nothing. Immeasurable Unnamable Nothing.*

*I float in it. It's a vacuum but there is energy in it. It's infinite and endless, but it's flat and immediate. It's pitch-black absolute zero but somehow has pulsing light and bubbling heat. It's void of void -- void even of the concept of void, yet full without feeling full. Grace, it is grace, amazing grace.*

*I put my hand into it and feel an edge; an edge that has no substance, no material presence, but still feels like an edge. I rise up and see it is an 'edge' to an egg-shaped opening into a passageway.*

*I grip the 'edge' to pull myself into the passageway and the edge has an infrared glow and I see the bones of my hand, as though looking at an x-ray.*

*My whole body becomes skeletal and I sweep into the passageway. Inside is a river and I race with it and there's another egg-shaped opening and a kind of spider-web ladder, but silky, not sticky. I start climbing the ladder and straightaway I stand awestruck in a great banquet hall full of feasting, celebrating people; laughing, singing, dancing, with rhythmic drums and fluting music everywhere. It is Carnival, a medieval faire, a children's garden and Fat Tuesday all in one. There are banners and flags, tapestries and mosaics, kaleidoscope clouds and coiling rainbows.*

*There is joy as far as I can see in every direction, but... no shadows spell time and no points place space.*

*A Little Person Spirit, the one I saw in the Burning Water Lodge, the one I first met when I was tied to the porch, emerges from mist and slowly materializes before me. He is my height and size; in this realm he is like me.*

*He has a string of 'buttons' with faces on them, which he holds up in front of me.*

*"What's that?"*

*"Your next life, pick one."*

*There are no words. Just mind reading mind.*

*I point to one that is about one third of the way from his left, my right, as mirrors work.*

*"That one. That actor," I say telepathically.*

*He laughs.*

<<< >>>

Someone had died and someone was not yet born, and yet both of us were now awake.

We were afraid, though, to open our eyes. We didn't want to see what we knew to be true. We knew we were lying in a bed that smelled of bleach and piss. We heard the hum of a machine and the steady beep--beep of time measured in seconds between each beep. We heard the soft swoosh of a small bellows. Suck in, suck out; suck in, suck out; we heard that.

We felt things in one arm, and when we moved that arm tubes moved with it. Something, a soft cloth, was wrapped around our head and something, a yoke with the texture of leather pressed on our chin.

And still that hook in our mouth and a weight on our tongue.

We couldn't talk, we couldn't move. If we opened our eyes would we know why we couldn't move? If we opened our eyes would we be paralyzed and, if so, how did that happen and who, which one of us -- the one that died or the one just born -- did that happen to? If we kept our eyes closed, it wouldn't be true.

They talked behind our back, sometimes in whispers. We heard the whispers. Our hearing was very good, better than ever. We could hear a pin drop.

They talked about an operation, an emergency.

"If you had left him in the regional hospital, he might have died," someone said. "He very likely would have had an aneurism."

A different voice said, "We got the blood clot, but fluid built up in his head. We drained it. He's stable now, but… if we have to drain again, it's more complicated and we need to go over that procedure with you. We need your permission. Also, he suffered some damage to the muscles in his left eye. It may cause astigmatism."

Fluid in our head? Is that what caused the throbbing, the fever, the journeys and the dreams? Damage to my left eye? Is this God's justice? Am I atoning for my mother?

"How will you do that? What's more complicated, I mean… and when? Right away, or…" a familiar voice said.

They didn't know. I could hear them and they didn't know what I knew. One of us had died and one of us had been born and both of us were awake.

"Let's go down the hall and look at the x-rays. It's easier to explain. Again, it may not be necessary."

Their voices faded, the words that buzzed like hornets around me walked out the door. Only the beeps and sucking sounds and the rhythm of gathering darkness remained.

I didn't sleep. Instead, I wondered.

I know we both dreamt of Franklin Delano Roosevelt and fire all around.

I know we both dreamt of an underground river. He followed it to a web of silk and I climbed the web to the stars.

He dreamt a banquet table in the House of God.

I dreamt of a Jokoa at a Carnival in the Lodge of Creating.

He enjoyed communion under the cross. I watched eagles pluck trout from spawning streams, yet... once we were whole. Once we found a horse nuzzling the Earth under an apple tree. We rode it together as one.

That was before _I_ was born, before _I_ emerged, before _I_ crossed the edge of sight.

That was before he died.

_I wished Gramma Minnie were there. She would explain why... why the one who died struggled so against the roots growing from my ribs and the wings in my throat, but I knew she wouldn't come. She wouldn't come, not as long as Mother was there. They didn't get along. While the steady rhythms of the sounds in the room lulled me into that floating place -- that suspended, twilight place between sleep and awake -- I wondered why. Why didn't they get along?_

When I woke again, my eyes opened, opened in spite of me. Was I ready for this, my opened eyes, my alone mind? The hospital room was not totally dark, maybe midnight dark with a moving shadow.

"You're awake!" There was a male figure in a white coat at the foot of the bed looking at a clip of papers. "You gave us quite a scare, young man. It's a good thing we caught that clot in time."

I didn't speak. I can't speak. With this thing in my mouth, I didn't even try to talk. Why bother? In the world that's real, talking was unnecessary.

"Does my head still drip blood on the floor?" my eyes asked him.

White Coat didn't hear my eyes. He set the papers on a table, moved closer, and adjusted something, the sheet or the blanket.

I couldn't move my head left or right to see, not that I wanted to see. He leaned toward me. His breath smelled like cheap Manischevitz wine.

"You bit your tongue, that's why there's a depressant in there. It's got to heal. Is it still sore? Never mind, I know you can't answer."

His put his Palmolive-hand on the ring around my neck.

"How does the neck brace feel?" He didn't look at my eyes for my answer. "We don't want you to move your head. Don't worry, you'll get used to it. We have to keep pressure off the incision."

He put a bottle on a hook above me, and a tube dropped onto my face. He grabbed that tube, pulled on one of the tubes in my arm, tugged on it, and then pushed on it. I heard two soft pops.

"Just rest. A nurse will come frequently to check on you. Tomorrow morning we'll take you for a ride down the hall."

Next thing I knew, Mother walked into the room. I could tell it was her by the sound of her timid, halting footsteps. Why did she walk as though all her sorrow was in the soles of her shoes?

"Visiting hours are over," Manischevitz-breath said to her. "You shouldn't be here."

"Dr. Leavitt gave me permission. I'm leaving in the morning. I thought I'd sit with him a while."

"I gave him a sedative. He'll be asleep soon, if he's not already."

"Thank you, I won't be long."

Manischevitz muttered "Very well" and turned away.

I smelled him leave.

I was alone with my mother. She smelled of currants and almonds. I felt her poetic past. I heard metal chair legs scrape the tile floor. She sat. On the edge of the bed her warm hands clasped at my hips. Were her hands gripped in prayer? I thought she was praying… until I heard her sobbing, weeping… almost grieving.

I kept my eyes closed and held my breath, even though I wanted to reach out and touch her, promise her I was not worth those surging tears. I wanted to, I cared, but I was anxious and, anyway, I couldn't move.

*I want to give you apples, peaches, and pears.* My mind said that.

I was recalling one of her poems she wrote in the journal she kept with her sheet music in the piano bench; the journal I snuck looks at when I was learning to read; the journal in which I hoped to read that she cared about me.

*'I want to give you apples, peaches, and pears, but it's wartime, and there are no gifts during wartime. I want to give you promises I won't break. I want – but it's wartime and everything breaks in wartime.'* How did that poem end? I don't remember. The mind of the one who died would remember. I must be in the mind of the one just born.

"Dear God," she said, inhaling hard, swallowing her tears. Ah, she *was* praying; crying and praying.

"Dear God, forgive me. I know … that I've… misplaced… this boy's childhood. I know I have. I can't change that now. I wish that I could. I would change so many things if I could."

"But I am changed, Mother, I am!" My brow was shouting. "I'm a new person; Jokoa gave me a new life! Mother, touch your fingertips to mine, and you will hear me!"

"He's my only child, Lord… of all my pregnancies he's the only one who lived. And now You've spared him again, You brought him back from the rim, and I… I thank You; with all my heart I thank You."

She stopped. Choked.

"I have to… go… away… leave him for a while. My father doesn't want…" She stopped again. "My mother is an invalid and we have to take her home."

She was explaining! You don't have to explain things to Spirit! Was she telling *me?* Did she know I could hear her?

Her forehead dropped onto the bed and her knuckles touched my hips and she cried so hard I couldn't stand it. If I weren't so groggy, so fighting against sleep, I would have bawled too, like a sad calf.

There was water in my eyes; I felt tears sneaking out from under my eyelids. Why couldn't she see the choke in my throat? I couldn't swallow it. It wouldn't go down. Oh no, it was the damn thing on my tongue.

"My life's a mess," she said and lifted her head. Her voice regained some calm, "and I don't know how to fix it. My dreams and goals are in splinters. I feel like I'm standing on a riverbank watching my life rush by out of control. Why doesn't my life reflect the sky? River be still. Please Lord God, please let the river be still. And... please Lord, let Hunter wake up with a sound mind and a sound body, and then let my father accept him into our house."

I smelled Manischevitz-breath come back into the room. He must have had more to drink.

"Thy Will be done," Mother finished.

"I'm sorry, Mrs. Koenig, but I must ask you to leave. If you wish to wait overnight in the lobby, that's okay, but we can't have visitors on the ward at this hour."

Mother took my hand with both her hands. A couple of our fingertips touched...

"I have to go..." she said, rocking my hand, "...back to Pennsylvania. But as soon as I can, I'll be back to visit. Thanksgiving, maybe we can have Thanksgiving together."

I called out to her through my fingertips:

"I hide, you know, in the back of my mind. I go there to thank the ancestors. I say to them, 'You know I know you're here.' I like my ancestors. I like to listen to their stories and dream _their_ dreams. And Mom..."

(I decided to call her Mom.)

"I know you know I'm here."

She squeezed my hand.

# 16

# *THE MOON OF THE LONGEST DARK*

Back in March 1951, during the annual condolence ceremony at the foot of a maple tree, Haksot explained to Nick and me that Death carries a black wand and that each time Death taps his black wand on the ground, an unborn's life is sucked away.

"Death is jealous of Life because Life is Eternal. Death isn't eternal. Clay People don't know that, even though there's words in the Bible that tell them that... 'a time to be born and a time to die...' Those are Earth People words. Whoever spoke those words knew Death is the opposite of birth, not the opposite of Life. Earth People know that Death is born again over and over."

"Aren't Clay People Earth People? Clay is Earth..." I asked.

"Clay People souls come from some joint called heaven. Their Creator came down and made a little clay doll and then breathed a Soul into it. Makes sense. Their Creator was a desert rat. Had no appreciation for the Earth. Worshipped the Sun. That's why Clay People are so warlike. The Sun... he likes the sound of war."

I looked up through freezing drizzle and saw a friendly smile in his eyes. He looked me back and said:

"Your soul is a prayer of the Earth. We see our ancestors around you. You have a Place of Emergence. Otherwise, you wouldn't be learning our ways.

"There's some words I'm gonna say now. I don't expect you to completely understand, but I do ask you to remember. These words have knowledge and are meant to protect both of you." He looked at Nick, then reached out and drew Nick close, "Because here at this condolence ceremony, Death is around and has spotted both of you.

"Death particularly likes unborn souls. Unborn souls have no defenses, 'specially if their mothers are lost souls.

"The black wand, it's hollow," he went on teaching. "Death taps that black wand – it makes a vital sound, a lustrous sound. That sound tricks unborn souls and persuades them to give away their longing for Life before they even draw first breath. Death sucks out that longing through the black wand and gets revitalized, even fortified.

"Death is a sorcerer; he also seeks innocent souls like you two, but living children he has to trick, deceive into thinking they are *getting* power.

"When your voices change and you grow some hair down there, we will initiate both of you, educate you how to keep the power of innocence. We will take each of you to the birthplace of your souls, your Place of Emergence. Once you reconnect with your soul's Place of Emergence, not only will you be protected but you will be able to choose the time and place of your death."

Nine months later on December 21, 1951, and only one month after I was out of the hospital, I saw Death's sorcerer-face for the first time. I knew the skulking figure I saw was Death because he held the black wand.

Every year at Christmas time, actually on the solstice night, Father and I delivered clothes and food and toys to needy families on the reservation. The toys and clothes were distributed in the form of a giveaway. Of course my father told the story of the First Christmas, but then he asked the traditionals, the old people including Haksot, to tell stories from the Onodowaga tradition; stories that were *only* told during the Moon of the Deepest Dark. That was more exciting than the manger scene as far as I was concerned.

After that Santa Claus would come and do the giveaway, only my father would introduce Santa Claus as a Sacred Clown. I really admired Dad for that.

It was about 4pm on December 21, 1951, and the dark was descending on that shortest of days. My father unlocked the front door of the Old Quaker House as I pulled presents out of the trunk. My arms full, just one month from my concussion and operation, I moved too fast, felt dizzy, stumbled and nearly fell. I caught my balance by looking for a horizon line, and saw down the road a mile or more east red flashing lights littering the white winter landscape and curling at me at high speed.

I stopped short, almost dropped the packages.

"Something's wrong."

Father had spotted it too. "Ambulance. Maybe there's an accident out on Route 20."

We both stood and watched as the ambulance approached, flew by us, and raced west; its screaming siren and painful lights bouncing off the dark grey sky and white-blanketed forest.

We waited for the lights to disappear down the hill past Old Town Road, but the lights didn't disappear. They turned right on Old Town Road, the road Gramma Minnie lived on.

"Let's go." Father was serious. He knew something. "Put the packages back in the trunk and get in the car."

When we got to the intersection in Old Town, Father turned right and drove toward the flashes we could see echoing in the enforcing dark. As we drove down the hill off the ridge, we knew for sure the trouble was at Gramma's house.

There's a long horseshoe shaped dirt road in from the asphalt that curls around the house. We saw the ambulance was parked facing us on the south curve and we didn't want to block it, so we came in from the north side and parked at the top of the bend near the main door of the house.

The ambulance driver and a nurse were bringing a gurney with a body on it down off the porch. The crew was having difficulty; the porch was icy, one half of it was stacked four-feet high with firewood, and there was foot-deep snow and a yard to cross.

My father literally ran from the car to the gurney to help. The crew recognized him and welcomed him. I wrapped my scarf around, and pulled my earflaps down, and trudged after him.

On the gurney Norma was all swathed in white sheets and blankets. Her face was ghostly pale. I feared she was dead, but then I recognized the bottle and a tube and a needle in her arm and knew otherwise. What I did know was that she lost her baby. I knew that because I saw Death hovering near. He wore a cloak of winter's shadows, he moved like a scythe, and he held the black wand.

A blink after I saw Death, something hit me in my gut. My stomach chucked acid into my throat. I swallowed at the bitter crud; it went partly back down. My gut chucked again and the acid came out my nose. I wipe the hot snot away with my mittens and spit the undone swallow into the snow.

The nurse at the front of the gurney pulled with one hand and held the bottle high with her other hand. The driver pushed from the tail of the gurney and, with my father on one side and Gramma on the other, the four of them plowed the gurney slowly through the snow.

The grey silhouette with the black wand shadowed the gurney like a panther.

*He had acquired the unborn. Was the mother next?*

My thought froze in the air; then was snapped like an icicle by sudden wailing keening. Oskee, on the porch in his day clothes, shattered the frigid silence.

*Oh, my God, he made such a mortal sound … He's deaf. Does he feel the sounds he makes*

Oskee pointed. His wailing turned to sobbing. He wasn't pointing at his mother. He saw Death too.

Haksot came out of the house with a coat for Oskee. The old man looked more care-worn than I had ever seen him. He made no attempt to "shush" Oskee. How do you "shush" a deaf child?

Nick, shivering, sucking air through chattering teeth and then blowing back warmth into his hands, stood beside Oskee. Nick didn't have boots on and his shoes and socks were soaked and old wool hand-me-down pants were so wet I could smell them.

Haksot's eyes, through cold tears, held a plea, "Not now… not again," even as teardrops struggled from them. One drop rolled to the tip of his nose, and then fell. Another took its place. Others dripped on his flushed cheeks.

Haksot's aching voice dragged my mind out from its stupid sidetrack. "I'll pierce and give flesh! I'll cut my hair. I'll sing 'kano:ta.'"

Haksot was lamenting, talking to Spirits, or Death, or both. He stepped off the porch and followed the gurney's track through the yard. I pulled my earflap hat tighter onto my head and tagged along behind him.

The nurse climbed into the ambulance behind the gurney that swaddled Norma. I saw Death right beside the gurney. Still, I had not seen him tap the black wand that sucks away life.

*Did it have to tap only on the Earth? Would it work inside the ambulance? Was the wand only for the unborn and the innocent?*

As if to answer ,Death looked me in the eye and bore his chilling grin into me.

The driver slammed shut the back door and hurried for the driver's seat.

"Wait! I need to go with you!" Gramma's hand was on the passenger door.

"It's not allowed, ma'am," the driver said as he got into his seat. The door shut, the motor gunned, the lugged rear tires spun momentarily in the snow, and the glinting lights brightened from the revving.

Gramma stepped back from the spitting slush.

"Norma! Be strong!" Her cry gaveled against the steel walls of the war surplus Red Cross Dodge.

The ambulance lurched and swayed in the rutted dirt road, red lights waving good-bye. A minute later, on the snow-packed asphalt, the siren screamed once more, and then crooned into the darkness, fading like a train's whistle.

"There was so much blood." Gramma looked at my father with anguish. "I couldn't stop the bleeding. I tried everything."

Gramma picked up and started wringing and twisting a blood-soaked towel that had fallen from the gurney.

"How did you contact them?" Father asked.

"Nick ran over to the neighbors."

"All the way to Old Town?"

"No…" She nodded in the other direction. "Hottis…"

"Ahhh…" my father said. "Hawks. Well, at least they made the phone call."

So that's why Nick's shoes and socks and pants were snow-soaked. The nearest neighbors were political, non-traditional foes in the reservation community. It was no surprise they had not shown up to help.

There was no family car – the Hudson hadn't run in months and certainly wasn't going to start on that cold December day. Mavis wasn't coming to pick up Nick until Christmas Eve. That was three days away. Gramma couldn't wait until then.

"We can take you, Gramma," I chirped. "There's plenty of room. You can even stay at our place over night if you have to."

Father and Gramma Minnie just looked at each other and smiled.

"Minnie, get what you need. I'll take you to the hospital. Hunt, get in the backseat," Father abruptly said.

"I want him here tonight," Haksot said suddenly.

"What for. It's Story Night. I'll drop him at the Quaker House, take Minnie to town, then come back."

"I got my reasons, ceremony reasons," Haksot muttered, then looked at me.

*He knows I saw Death. He knows I saw the black wand. He has to do ceremony to clear all the dark matter.*

Gramma had been looking at me and then she said to my father, "He's right. Hunter should stay here tonight. I'll explain later. I'll just be a minute."

"I don't agree. For… custody reasons…"

"Call Mavis," Haksot said to Gramma, ignoring my father. "Tell her to get over here tomorrow. She can take us to town. We'll all give blood."

All of a sudden Death, holding the black wand, appeared from the pitching swirling sky. The sight of him made me dizzy again. I fell to my knees. I clawed through the snow to the frozen ground for a handhold.

Cold and close, he whispered: *Of course you can see me. I want you to see me. You are my friend. The black wand has power; it is a medicine, a hollow bone. Twirl it; it spins straw into gold. Blow through it; it weaves songs from the wind.*

His words hissed from beyond bony teeth and a lipless smile.

*Take hold of the black wand. It will give you the power of life and death. You already have blood on your hands. Your sister, Norma's baby -- take the wand now and Norma will live.*

Death wanted me to hold the wand. Death called me to be the angel. I pulled off my gloves and grabbed the wand.

"I'll do it! I'll do it!" I gasped.

Silence, quiet as a leafless tree, was Death's response.

I opened my eyes. I held a branch from the black walnut tree in my hands. Its icy grain made my whole being shudder. I felt a skip in my heart.

Gramma, my father, Haksot, Nick all stared at me, frightened, worried, stunned. Only Oskee was not upset. He knelt beside me and, like a loving puppy, put his left arm around my shoulders. Little Oskee, the deaf child, the fetal alcohol child, the retarded child, saw what I saw, somehow heard what I heard.

He took the branch from my chapped, bleeding hand. He waved the black stick in the air to all four directions. His voice boomed, "Kahsah!" four times.

"Kahsah!" It means "all eaten up." It was a sound made to placate any evil spirits that were around. Oskee was saying, "Go away, there's nothing here for you."

He must have remembered the word from the time before he caught the scarlet fever that deafened him.

"Grandson, stand up," Haksot said softly, tenderly. "It's all right, you've had a vision."

He turned to Nick. "Go stoke the fires in the stove and the potbelly. Get it warm. And get the mask down from my bedroom wall." He turned to Gramma. "Hurry, get your things and go. Norma needs you."

"Wait!" my father begged. "What's going on? What's he going to do?"

"It's all right," Gramma said.

"But he's *my* son, he's… what's Haksot going to do?"

"He's going to blow fire and talk to the one who's listening."

"The one who's listening? What do you mean?"

"I'll explain in the car. Please, let us take care of it. You'll see him tomorrow."

"Minnie, I can't do that. You know I can't. The Judge already thinks he's unbalanced. If it got out you're doing ceremonies for him because he's hallucinating… I can't, not now, not this time."

"If you don't, you'll lose him for…" Haksot muttered aloud, but Gramma put up her hand and silenced the old man with that look nobody ever crossed.

"Hunter, get in the car," she sighed.

"Eni:a'iehûk! S`hondowêk'owa!" Haksot cried out as we drove away.

I didn't know what that meant and Gramma wasn't saying, but it didn't sound good.

# 17

## *THE DEAD DON'T PRAY*

"Wake up! It's gettin' dawn." Haksot shook my shoulder.

I rolled over and looked out the window of Nick's room. It was early, all right; sunlight in the eastern sky barely pierced a fitful drizzling rain.

"Wha? What's the matter?"

"The Dead don't pray; only the near-dead. I need your help." With that Haksot turned to go back down the stairs. "There's hot cocoa on the stove. Get dressed. Put on rain gear. We need to hurry."

*Why me?* I thought, but knew not to ask out loud.

Ten minutes later, covered in rain gear, I followed Haksot's determined shuffle down the road towards Old Town.

"From the looks of things, it musta rained all night," I yawned while trying to make conversation. "Good thing they finally paved this road."

"Don't talk. Pray. It starts now." Haksot pointed at a lone Musclewood Tree in the southwest corner of Tilo Mantooth's cornfield on the flats at the foot of the ridge.

"Climb to the top. Cut four branches round as your little finger and this long..." he indicated from my elbow to my wrist. He handed me an ancient flint knife with a smooth bone handle.

I picked my way through a dense blackberry thicket to the base of the tree.

At the base of the tree, I unsnapped my rain slicker and then removed my boots, leaving my shoes and socks in the boots. There was no way I was gonna bear-hug my way to the first crotch wearing the slicker; plus I knew I needed to be barefoot. I'd climbed Musclewood before, but never in the rain.

My first two tries failed. Not only was the surface slick, but also blackberry vines had wrapped around the trunk. My hands and arms were stung twenty times.

I looked back at Haksot.

"Pray harder," he barked. Then he began to sing a tune I had never heard before. The words were 'old language' and I didn't understand a single word.

I took a deep breath and concentrated on blending with the tree. The rain suddenly let up. I wrapped around that trunk, thorns and all, and bellied up eight feet to the first crotch. After that it was easier. Haksot didn't stop singing until I got near the top.

It was three weeks past Easter, 1952. All the drama of Norma's miscarriage had slowed to a crawl and she had actually gotten her life together and was working full time down in Salamanca at tribal headquarters.

I had been questioned by lawyers and doctors and gave what they called a deposition just after my twelfth birthday. There was something called a custody hearing that had been re-scheduled after first my father and then the

Judge, my mother's father, appealed and we were waiting to hear about when that would happen.

During Easter week I went once again with Haksot in the night of the full spring moon to count the northbound-silhouetted herons migrating the resurrecting sky. Nick was with us that night and the next day. Then, Nick helped roast and mash the horse chestnuts we had picked the previous fall to be used to paralyze the bait-frogs.

When I arrived the following Saturday, the day to trap hammerheads that spawned in the tributaries of the Katakeskea River, I found Haksot in the barn harnessing the horses to an old hay wagon. Oskee was sitting on the back of the wagon. Oskee greeted me in sign language and I greeted in turn. I looked around for Nick.

"It's visiting day at the prison. All of a sudden Mavis has decided Nick needs to get to know his father," Haksot answered when I asked why Nick wasn't around.

I shrugged. That whole situation bewildered me. All I knew was that Mavis was seventeen when Nick was born and that his father went to prison a couple years after that.

"Nick's father gets out soon and Mavis figures if he gets a job, he can provide child support. So all the sudden she's been going to visit and making Nick go too," Haksot grumbled.

"But they're not married."

"Doesn't matter. Law says he has to provide."

"What happens if he doesn't?"

"Depends. I s'pose he could go back to prison."

"But if he's in prison, he can't provide child support. That doesn't make sense."

"Grandson, a lot of things in this world don't make sense. And sometimes I think you're too smart for your own good. Hop on, you're going to have to work the brake."

I perked up at that. I'd never worked the brake before.

"What about Oskee?" I asked, jumping up while Haksot used a box as a step to climb onto the wagon.

"We have to take him. Minnie's got some argument with the tribal council at the headquarters and Norma is working. The hammerheads are running, there's a break in the rains, it's now or never. It won't be easy, I tell ya; I wish Nick was here."

The wagon had no seat. It did have a headache bar, a kind of fence on hay wagons that kept a load from sliding forward onto the person driving the horses, especially if the brake failed on a downhill.

Oskee sat on the back and dangled his feet from the end and hummed the songs he heard in his heart.

We went up the ridge, through Old Town, and then crossed the east-west reservation road and continued onto a firebreak that was at least a mile long through the forest. The firebreak led down to the river. The break was more a big meadow than a man-made break. It was green and pretty with wild flowers and glistening with snow run-off from the shadowed forest slopes. There were bees and birds and bird songs. It was spring. It was spawning season. It was heaven.

At the end of the break there was a large crescent-shaped pond. The north end was shallow and was the place where we drugged the frogs. At the south end, the pond got deeper, and at the tip off the crescent, a reinforced wooden lock shuttered a catch-basin. In the heavy spring run-off, water was sloughing over the top of the lock into a drainage ditch and then over a 30-foot cliff into the Katakeskea River.

To the right, maybe fifty yards through a thick tree line, was the deep gully that funneled Little Ghost Creek into the river. Little Ghost Creek was prime spawning ground for hammerheads.

"You take the bucket and the chestnuts and get started," Haksot said, whipping the reins around the headache bar, but giving the horses enough slack to chew on the greens in the firebreak. "Get four frogs to start. I'll bait the traps, you take them to the creek and get them in the water before the frogs die. Once they're in the water they'll start kicking again and that draws the hammerheads. I'll collect the rest."

"What about Oskee?" I asked as I watched the eight year-old run into wet grass after a white butterfly.

"Oskee will try to save the frogs. Keep an eye on him. Don't let him near the gully."

There are such steep slopes down to Little Ghost Creek and it is so overgrown that from the top of the bank I had to work each trap, one by one, down the sharp slopes, monkeying from sapling to sapling down and up. At the edge of the creek I lashed each trap with a long line to a tree or sapling and then slipped the traps into the fast-moving creek.

While I was gone with the first four, Haksot began drugging the frogs and baiting the traps. Only when he saw me coming back from each run did he then bait the next set. He wanted the frogs to be as fresh as possible.

At first I lashed four traps together and dragged them as quick as possible from the wagon to the creek, starting near the mouth. I worked up a sweat and was breathing hard. I should have dragged with only two traps each time, but I was trying to impress. I lost track of Oskee, although once I did see him from the corner of my eye wading around in the pond. He hadn't tried to follow me. He was more concerned with the frogs in the pond.

I found the last four traps baited and waiting on the wagon. I looked around, then walked around and found Haksot and Oskee lying on a patch on sun-dried grass on the other side of the wagon, where Haksot let the horses graze. I imagine Oskee was a handful for the old man; probably that was why Haksot was tired.

I had set twelve traps; each one further upstream. Dragging four traps 70 yards to the last point upstream was daunting. I was exhausted. I decided to take two.

When I came back to the wagon for the final two traps, the baited frogs were gone.

I figured Oskee had set them free. I went around the wagon to tell Haksot and scold Oskee. Haksot was sleeping and Oskee wasn't there.

I could see the whole pond. There were a few frogs and small fish floating out in the middle, but no Oskee in sight.

A sinking feeling hit my stomach. If Oskee followed me to the creek, maybe to put the last two frogs into the water, or worse to let frogs free from some of the set traps, he... I didn't want to think about it.

In frenzy I shook Haksot awake.

"Where's Oskee?"

"Huh, huh?" Haksot flailed his arms to stop me from shaking him.

"He's gone. Oskee's gone." I was screaming. "He took the last two frogs." I pointed at the traps.

Haksot fumbled to his feet, looked around, rubbed his eyes, looked at the pond, then grabbed me by both shoulders and glared: "You fool! I told you to keep an eye on him!"

Stung by his word, fearful sweat dripping out of me, hysterical, I shook my head, "I don't know, I don't know" and let a wave of guilt tremble me. Then, I turned toward the creek, wrestled free, and ran. I never ran so fast. Nothing bothered me; not the brush, the undertow of twisted logs, the vines, or the whipping branches. Nothing slowed me. I ran a straight line to where I set the first trap.

Nothing, no sign he had been there, no footprints, no slips in the mud aside from my own trail down.

I never felt so sick since when I saw what the bull did to my mother.

I took off for the creek mouth, skirting brush piles, jumping logs, and trampling cattails. If somehow he had fallen in Little Ghost and if somehow his body made it into the main course of the Katakeskea, the deep channel would pull it under and it would be in Lake Erie in three hours. If he had fallen in anywhere upstream, I had to try to beat him to the creek mouth.

When I got to the delta-shaped pool of the creek mouth, I saw his shirt, I recognized his shirt; I saw just his shirt in the water of the creek mouth twenty feet below. Then I saw the slip and the slide of something, someone having lost footing and gone down the bank.

I stood there, screaming his name, screaming, screaming, "Oskee! Oskee!" as loud as I could, wailing the way he wailed, frustrated, knowing he was deaf, knowing calling his name did no good.

I slid down the bank, hit the water, pitched forward, tripped on a root, grabbed splashing water, and somehow got to my feet. The water was moving fast, scary fast, and up near my armpits. His shirt was snagged on a fallen tree branch. When I unhooked it, I nearly lost my footing on the slick shale creek bottom.

I stood in that creek looking upstream toward the twenty yards inland where I had set the first trap. It was so overgrown and dense; but I was hoping... even though I was holding his shirt I was hoping.

I stood there, helpless and hysterical, holding his shirt, until I heard Haksot call my name from the bank above.

Haksot pushed the old horses as fast as they would go until we got to the General Store in Old Town. He went inside and called the reservation police.

Seven hours later the rez cops retrieved the body from New York State troopers and brought Oskee home in the back of a truck. He was stuffed feet first into a large burlap sack. No perfumed hearse, no whiskey-soured undertaker. It was reservation way. They bury their own.

That's why I was in that Musclewood tree in a drizzling rain the next morning. Skeletal soaked, I cut those several smooth branches with an old flint knife — a prized possession of the famous family of flintknappers named One Knife; a flint knife older than the turtle shell rattles and the False Face Masks that hung on the wall in the parlor; a flint knife kept in a one-hundred-year-old maple chest on an ancestral altar. I was in that tree that late April day in 1952 because the body of Little Dry Hand One Knife lay in a pine box on a table in that same parlor with the turtle rattles and the false faces.

Little Dry Hand, aka Oskee, aka 'Snot,' eight-years-old, deaf and retarded no more, instead bloated and blue and starting to stink from the silt waters of Little Ghost

Creek where we set the fish traps for the hammerheads that spawn in the springtime -- drowned trying to save frogs.

<<< >>>

"The dead don't pray. The near-dead, 'Jiskweh' the 'ghost minder', prays for them." Gramma was standing on a ladder and her head and arms were in the eave above her bedroom.

"He skewers his chest with the smooth sticks from a Musclewood Tree. He conducts 'Okiweh,' the four-day 'Prayer for the Dead'." She intoned this information at me without audible emotion.

I stood at the foot of the ladder and one by one she handed me boxes she had stored in the eave.

"On the first morning we attach a feathered eagle claw to each Musclewood stick skewered in his chest. We wrap him in wolf robes and seat him on the hide of a deer. The hair on the hide must have white tips; that is, it must be an old buck. The Jiskweh sits at the gravesite and prays four days for the one that died; the one who no longer prays for itself. At night he sleeps on his back. The claws are sharp. If he moves about too much they will cut him."

"Imagine," she said, looking down at me and bending her hand three fingers down and the thumb behind, "the talons can drill into the heart of a rabbit or even a kit fox."

She pulled loose a very old trunk or suitcase and nearly fell backward with it. Slowly she eased it step by step down the ladder.

"If the Jiskweh does not conduct the Okiweh, both the dead and the living are affected, sometimes harmfully. If a soul is not set free to be judged by Jicosahse; if a soul is snagged with self, then that 'not-yet spirit' can create grim trouble for the living."

She set the trunk on the bed and opened it slowly as though not to disturb the dust on top. She checked on the item inside by touching it ever so gently. It was a deer hide and the hair on the hide had white tips. Satisfied, she closed the trunk.

"At the end of the four days, the Jiskweh is purified in a Burning Water Lodge and then we have a feast. We always have a feast..." Her voice tailed off.

"Take the boxes into the kitchen. I'm right behind you."

In the kitchen she laid out embroidered cloth and beaded items on the table.

"The Jiskweh cries for all of us. He speaks his prayers with tears. Tears carry the dead on their journey home," Gramma said. "We call it that journey, 'Kahatiyako:oh,' 'Crossing the Woods'."

Gramma sorted through embroidered cloth and buckskin breeches and fringed coats in the boxes from the eave. She very carefully set aside several beaded belts after inspecting the markings and lengths.

I knew something about beaded belts. Haksot had gone on a rant once about how the belts were sacred and different belts told different stories:

"There's a song and a story and a legacy in every stitch," he growled. "But the 'make-it-up as they go' Clay People call them wampum! Then they translate wampum as money! Goddamn Clay People. Wampum means ember, the fire inside a fire."

Right after Oskee's body was brought back to us, Haksot began to hone eagle claws he had stored in a

parfleche hanging on a peg in the barn. He used a hog strap dipped in corn oil and weltered in sand to hone the claws.

That's why Haksot needed those smooth tree branches. That's why I was in the musclewood tree in Tilo Mantooth's cornfield.

Oskee was wrapped in hand-made ornamental, embroidered buckskin, beaded moccasins, and was bound by a beaded belt that told the story of his clan. He was laid out for one day in an open pine box on a plain wood table in the parlor with turtle rattles and false-face masks and some of Oskee's finest sketches of frogs on the walls.

Heavy plumes of cedar rose continuously from the coals in the Studebaker hubcap at the foot of the table. During that night the pine box was closed. The next morning he was taken in the box on the wagon to the forest northeast of the house. He was taken from the pine box and gently placed in a hand-dug grave under a maple tree. He was fitted into the big roots and was covered with stones from the creek that swept him away.

The men who went for the stones brought back the traps. The captured hammerheads were gutted and filleted and became a part of the feast.

At sundown of the burial day, the Okiweh began. There were at least a hundred people there; mostly Wolf Clan, some Hawk Clan, two rez cops, and a few people from town, including my father. There were traditional 'Spirit-is-in-Charge', 'Ours-is-not-to-Reason-Why' eulogies Seneca-style, and dust-to-dust ashes-to-ashes speeches Christian-style. There were a lot of songs, some in the old language, some of them in the modern Seneca, and even one hymn, Amazing Grace, sung in English and in Seneca.

The grand old man on the reservation, Kanojaohweh -- his name means "Big Kettle" -- made the flint knife incisions into Haksot's chest. He pinched and numbed and wadded the wrinkled flab of skin above the nipple; then pushed in the flint arrowhead, sharper than Swedish steel, and made just the right size triangular cut.

Kanojaohweh, eighty, maybe ninety years old, still clear-eyed, had the knowhow. The flint was so sharp the old man's bony fingers had no trouble carving two vertical incisions. When the arrowhead tip poked through the far side of each wad of skin, two pencil-thin, smooth Musclewood branches – green with youth but tough as veterans, one in each incision – were pushed back through the cuts as the flint arrowhead scalpel was pulled out.

The deer hide was spread out and the claws attached to the skewers and then the wolf robes were wrapped round. The ritual began. Haksot would sit and sleep beside the grave the next four days.

"That was extraordinary," my father said as we drove back that night to our house in town.

"I grew up with the Seneca and I've worked with them for more than fourteen years, but that was the first traditional funeral ceremony I've ever been to. Imagine, there you are, age twelve, a non-Indian, and they asked you to climb the tree and cut the branches that pierced through the flesh of an Elder's chest so he could help his great grandson 'cross the woods' to the Spirit world. Every nuance of their ceremonies are sacred to them, so for you to be a part of that…"

He patted me on the shoulder, but it didn't make me feel better. I kept thinking, *I didn't save Oskee; I didn't kill him but I didn't save him. If I'd just paid more attention. If I hadn't been so full of myself…*

# 18

## *WE ALWAYS*
## *MAKE A FEAST*

"Why do they always make a feast?"

There's no response.

"Dad?"

"What? Oh, beg pardon, I was lost in thought. What did you say?"

"Why do they always make a feast? I know at a Christian funeral people eat afterwards, but the Seneca... they started making fry bread and cakes four days ago. They're gonna feed anyone who walks in the door!"

Father laughed. "They have a feast in order to ensure... it's a way of saying that Oskee's life is not over. He just went back to where he came from."

"The other side of the woods..."

"The other side of the woods..."

"The feast is tonight, right, after they bring Haksot in?"

"Sundown."

"Why are you taking me back now?"

"Minnie asked for you. She said she needs your help. I'll take you as far as the Quaker House. You can walk the back trail from there. I've got to be at the state hospital and then at the lawyers. I'll be out tonight for the feast and to pick you up. You will not be staying the night. Anyway, you've got school tomorrow. You can't miss two days over this. People will talk."

We could see the Indian School about a mile distant, and when we drove around the next left bend we'd see the Quaker House too, on the other side of the road.

"People will talk – you said that to Gramma when she wanted me to stay that night after Norma lost her baby."

Father waited until the Quaker House came into view before he answered. "Yes, people will talk. What do you know about that?"

"Nothing -- Haksot wanted to do ceremony, blow fire, cause I saw Death and I held the Black Wand. When Haksot sharpened the eagle claws the other night, he told me if he had done that ceremony, Oskee might still be alive."

"Haksot blamed you? That's not fair."

"I didn't kill Oskee, Dad; I just didn't save him."

"Have you considered why Haksot sharpened the eagle claws? I think he's doing penance. And he's wrong to make you feel guilty."

"What's penance?"

"It's, ah... self punishment."

"Anyway, you said I couldn't stay for him to blow fire because 'people will talk,' and at the White Hotel you said, 'don't say anything to Mother about spending time on the reservation.' You said, 'just because they're Indians, the law would go against you'."

"I did say that, yes."

"I figure that's what people will talk about, tell the law about, that I spend time with the Indians and somehow that is wrong. And yet, every time you're busy or going somewhere, you let me stay there. Doesn't make sense..."

Father pulled into the gravel parking lot in front of the old Quaker House. He left the engine running and the heater going against the morning fog from the lake, and then unbuttoned his suit coat and loosened his tie.

"You're right," he said, "about the custody case, but the talk is not just because Minnie is an Indian."

"Why do you call her Minnie? You and Haksot... everybody else calls her Gramma, even Father Justus called her 'Gramma'!"

Father turned to me so suddenly, his elbow hit the car horn and the sound startled not only the two of us but crows in the trees towards the river. A whole flock burst out, circled, and came back.

Father laughed at himself, settled back in his seat, and looked relieved.

"You know that State Teacher's College in Freeland?"

I nodded, I knew about it. Freeland was a large town south of Crystal Springs.

"Years ago, up until 1936, it was a boarding school/trade school for all the teen-age Iroquois kids who lived west of the Finger Lakes. Minnie lived there for three years in the mid-1920's; she was a music student and a dancer. She had a beautiful voice."

"Yeah, when she cooks ceremonial food, she sings to the food. She has a pretty voice, not nasal like the other clan mothers. Some of those women, when they sing, they sound like an electric saw..."

"Indian boarding schools were like reformatories. If she wanted to see her parents, they would have to come see her."

"That's not fair."

"The government knew if the kids went home to visit, they wouldn't come back, so they weren't allowed to leave. Even so, many of the older kids learned to sneak away, Minnie too, but not to see their families. Freeland was a dry town because of the boarding school. So the older ones would sneak out, jump a train or maybe someone had access to a car, and they would come to Crystal Springs, it's only ten miles, to my grandfather's bar, Sully's Bar, to drink and dance."

"Didn't they get arrested?"

"There was no drinking age then. Anybody could drink if the barkeep would serve him or her, and your great grandfather, David O'Sullivan from County Kerry, Ireland, would've served a baby in a carriage if it had the money. That sounds bad, but on the other hand, he was the only one in that family who didn't shun me."

"Wow! You've known Gramma since high school? How old were you?"

"Eighteen. She was seventeen."

"Seventeen? But... that's when she had Mavis."

Father quietly watched the last of the fog clear from the windshield, and then he said, "Yeah, that's when she had Mavis."

"So her husband was at the boarding school too?"

"No, she met Tom later."

"Then how...?"

"Minnie was expelled when she got pregnant. She went home to give birth, and there she stayed ever since."

"She likes to say she sleeps in the room she was born in."

"Then, when *Mavis* was seventeen she had Nick. After that, people started calling Minnie 'Gramma'; it gave her... respectability."

"Except you and Haksot... "

"I just want you to understand."

"What?"

"When the custody hearing comes up in court, you will hear rumors, gossip, stories. Both lawyers will ask you pointed questions. They're going to ask you if you've ever seen me be affectionate toward Minnie. Tell the truth."

"They asked me that in the deposition."

"Really? How did you answer."

"I said 'No'."

We sat in the car and watched the sun steam the morning dew off the roof of the old Quaker House. Maybe I should have paid more attention to what he was talking about, but I had something else on my mind.

"I don't want to walk the back trail. I'm afraid."

"Afraid. Why? You've walked it dozens of times."

"But not like now."

"Because..."

"Some Indians blame me for Oskee's death... Haksot called me a fool for not keeping an eye on Oskee."

"You're not responsible. It wasn't your fault. If Haksot called you a fool, he was calling himself a fool. The fact that he sat up for four days at the gravesite at his age means he blames himself," Father interrupted.

"He did take it back, but he said I was defenseless. He said Death had its eye on me, too. He told me not to walk the back trail."

"For God's sake, what does the back trail have to do with anything?"

"If I take the back trail feeling so weak and I see the Blacktail Deer again… what if I can't resist if she beckons?"

"Oh, Hunter… what Blacktail Deer stories have you been told?"

"Gramma told me if I'm in the woods and the Blacktail Deer calls, that she's very hard to resist, but that I should never, ever follow her."

"Blacktail Deer don't even live in this part of the country. They only live in the Rocky Mountains and out west."

"But I saw one. She beckoned me… by the quicksand, by the hedgerow… remember, I told you that."

"Hunter, that was a dream!"

"The dream was the Gatekeeper and the quicksand. But before that, we were walking to school and I saw a Blacktail Deer."

"Hunt, you know you see things."

"But that's when Gramma warned me about them!"

"Minnie was teaching you to be careful."

"Exactly… if no physical ones live here, it could only be a Spirit. That's why it's so tempting, and so dangerous!"

"Hmm… she's really…" Father put his foot on the clutch, put the Chevy in first gear, and pulled out onto the highway.

"Really what?"

He looked at his rear-view mirror before he answered. Then, "Clever…" is all he said.

"Where we going?"

"You got enough on your mind. I don't want you to worry. I'll just take you."

"Let 'em talk," I laughed.

"That's right," he answered. "Let 'em talk. They will anyway."

We drove in silence one of the two miles to the turn in Old Town. I just gazed out the window and studied the changes Spring brought to the forest. During the last mile, though, something was very wrong.

"That whole grove – all those trees – they're all dead. Look! Right next to them they're getting buds, and all of a sudden all these trees are dead."

"Dutch Elm disease. It's a fungus, comes in from the roots."

"But back there they were fine."

"The ones back there, the State came and injected a fungicide. This side of the rez is all traditional people, and they wouldn't allow it; so now all these trees are dying. All this land along here – the old man, Big Kettle, the one who pierced Haksot – this is all his and his relatives' land. They wouldn't allow the fungicide."

After we turned the corner at Old Town and reached the top of the ridge, Father slowed down almost to a stop. Then he did the most remarkable thing I've ever seen him do. He shoved in the clutch and slipped the Chevy out of gear. He wet two fingers with a lick of his tongue, gripped the steering wheel with two hands, and said, "I've wanted to do this for twenty years."

He steered the Chevy to the center of the road and muttered "Hang on."

We just flew down that steep straightaway. We could see all the way out that straight road. Good thing there were no other cars or wagons. I was so amazed and thrilled I didn't even glance at the speedometer.

We zoomed past the Musclewood Tree in Tilo Mantooth's field. Even on the flats we cruised out of gear, slowing down all the way to the north entrance of the loop road to Gramma's house.

I never knew he had that in him, but I was happy for him. I realized he had just released twenty years of something he had pent up inside.

There were ten cars parked on the south side of the driveway loop, half of them on the grass. Men and women I didn't recognize were carrying trays of food across the lawn. Father pulled into the north side to the barn entrance, then turned around and lined up to drive out the north road before he turned off the engine.

"The community is gathering... there's going to be a big crowd here tonight." Father nodded at one of the couples carrying a big tray of food. "Jimmy Shongwa and his wife... relatives of the Old Man, Big Kettle. They live over west of Old Town, near where the bridge crosses Little Ghost."

"Do you know them?"

"Long House People." Father points at an old man sitting on the porch, "Charlie Turtle... I think he's a False Face healer."

"How do you know so much?"

"I've lived around here most of my life and worked here on the rez the last fourteen years."

As I opened the door to get out of the car, my father touched my shoulder.

"Son, don't be surprised if some of the people here, maybe even a lot of the people here, are rude to you. The old people and the traditionals; they carry hundred-year-old grudges. Fourteen years and there are still a lot of people who don't like me. Just do whatever Gramma wants and don't take it personal, okay? I'll be back tonight."

I walked over to the house. Norma and Mavis were sitting on the porch, smoking. When they saw me, I smiled and went to greet them, and... they turned their backs to me. I wasn't expecting that from them. Not only that, all the rest of the afternoon they deliberately ignored me.

Gramma and three other women were busy in the kitchen, cooking a boatload of food. I stuck my head in the door and looked around.

Gramma saw me and immediately said; "You have to build the fire for the Burning Water. Get everything together. Don't expect help. Nick will not be ready."

She wiped her hands on a towel and walked up to me and in a lower voice said, "It's going to rain. You know what to do, right? Everything you need is in the barn. Go now."

"What do you mean, Nick won't be ready?"

"Grandson, you're on your own today. Don't be surprised if no one talks to you. It's part of the ritual. Until Haksot comes in and we know Oskee is safe on the other side, we keep talk to a minimum."

While she was talking I heard in the background one of the women mutter just loud enough, "What's he doin' here?"

Another answered, talking soft with words I couldn't hear.

During the afternoon, as I went back and forth from the barn to the fire pit, mourners gathered in the parlor or on the porch or waited leaning against their cars. By sundown there were easy 150 people there. Not one of them spoke to me.

An hour before sundown, I had the fire ready to light and the lodge covered with blankets and tarps. I could feel rain was close; I checked the leaves in the trees and many had turned over, so I covered the unlit fire with another tarp and went back to the kitchen carrying a shovel.

Outside a man with what looked like a canoe paddle was stirring a stew cooking in a horse trough that sat on cement blocks over a fire in a pit. Four other men were rigging a small rectangular canopy with poles and army tarps. They figured it was going to rain too.

The three women in the kitchen with Gramma were making biscuits, chopping vegetables, soaking dried fruit, peeling potatoes, opening mason jars, doing stuff.

"What's that for?" one of the women asked, looking at the shovel.

"Coals to start the fire," I stammered. I wasn't used to the coldness towards me.

Gramma nodded at the oven door. "Go ahead."

Before I opened the oven door, I watched Gramma sear some deer heart pieces, scoop them up with a spoon, drain the oil, and drop the seared pieces in a soup pot already bubbling with fresh wild onions and dried white turnips.

"Gramma," I blurted, "Am I Hath:o?"

She stopped, ladle in midair, and looked at me. The other three women, I didn't know them by name, stared at me. From the stricken look on all those faces, you'd think it's Gramma's own heart she was cutting up and ladling into the fry pan.

"Do you know what that means?" she asked.

"Angel of Death," I nodded.

She put the last of the deer heart in the pot and stirred before she said, "Well, it means 'The One Who Freezes the Heart.' Why do you ask?"

"I hear the talk. People saying things behind my back that they want me to hear." I eyed the other three women.

"What was said?"

I recited: "Norma's baby dies from 'never born.' The boy is 'in the house.' Oskee drowns at the fish traps. The boy is 'in the house.' The boy sees the Black Wand. He sees Death. It's a straight line. That's what was said."

My eyes filled with tears. "What do they mean, it's a straight line?" I wiped the tears away and blurted, "Gramma, I didn't kill him... I just didn't save him!"

"No, Hunter, you didn't kill him. Nobody thinks that."

"Am I gonna be sent away?"

Gramma put down her ladle, wiped her hands on her muslin apron, took me by the hand, and led me to the table. She sat down and nodded for me to do the same.

"You are not an Angel of Death," she said with decisiveness, "but since you had that dream and the Gate Keeper let you live, the Elders have counseled what to do about you. Haksot and I are willing to teach you, but there are some who caution against any outsiders learning our ways, even though *you* earn your keep.

"Given what's happened, there are many who say you should go, not because they blame you. It's just, they call you a wrinkle in the air... like distant thunder. 'Give it a rest,' they say to us.

"Just know that any decision made about you is based on what the Spirit says. It has nothing to do with what I feel, or Haksot thinks, or what Big Kettle says is best for the people."

She looked out the window.

"It's gonna rain any minute. Go, get the fire started."

"Is Nick...?"

"Nick is in his room. Leave him be. In the same way babies sometimes have to cry heavy before going to sleep, people who grieve alone, the grief will not end until they are exhausted. Nick is grieving alone.

"Get your coals and get the fire up. Keep it going in the rain and things will settle out for you."

Clay People have ways to keep a fire going in the rain, of course; the way of diesel fuel and gasoline. But in the traditions of Earth's Old Men, "backhanders" (as they call gas and diesel) are not allowed.

War surplus hemp rope, frayed into fine strands, is the fire-start. We aren't allowed to use matches, much less cigarette lighters. A spark from flint on steel or a coal from the stove and a whoosh of breath, and the frayed hemp flares up.

Handfuls of dry willow bark combined with straw from the barn floor kindle the burn. Long strips of birch bark, which burn even when wet, circle the stones set chimney-style on a log platform. Pine logs from a covered, dry stack finish the build.

I stack the logs tipi style, the way I was taught. That way, even in sheets of rain, the fire's vertical thermal bends the rain away.

<<< >>>

At sundown Haksot was lifted, frail and drained, from the brown with white-tipped deer hide, and set on his feet. The wolf robes fell loose, the eagle claws were loosened, and the skewers cut free. He was given chunks of scalded deer heart to eat. A young rez "nephew" helped Haksot walk to the circle of the eight pine trees where the Burning Water Ceremony took place. Nick was still nowhere in sight.

I was there, poking the fire, heating the stones to burn the water that would wash clean the residue of the "Okiweh" from Haksot's soul.

I stood, waiting; a twelve-year-old among seven very old men, Big Kettle, Jimmy Shongwa and Charlie Turtle among them, trying to read their thoughts, but knowing full well there was no way I could penetrate their minds.

They spoke their language the "old way." It's such a nasal language, I swear the old men didn't even move their lips. Instead, sounds seemed to move through their noses and off the roof of their mouths and through their top row of teeth, what they had left of teeth. The old words also had throat stops, or they spooled out from a cluck of the tongue. I hardly recognized a word. Modern Seneca had lost all of that old quality.

The six skinny, wrinkled, and weathered old men, two of them who had been in my first and only Burning Water Lodge, with pretend indifference watched me tend the fire, while the seventh, Haksot, was too spent to pay much attention.

They sat on benches in a lean-to shelter out of the rain. Waiting nearby was a wobbly, bent-willow structure, the Burning Water Lodge, covered by oily-smelling army tarps. East of the lodge was an altar, which was a small mound of dirt covered with eagle down, forlorn with rain-soak. Further east was the fire, the one I built, packed with sixteen big stones. Circling the lodge, the altar, and the fire was a grove of eight white pines planted many years ago.

Tobey, the twenty-something nephew, assumed he needed to supervise me. I didn't need supervision. Nick and I were taught well how to build fires and heat stones for Burning Water. I probably knew more than Tobey did, but he can't let on that was so. He was twenty-plus and I was twelve, and he had face to save.

The secret ingredient was dry incense cedar. Fire loves cedar. Fire will stay alive to eat cedar. Coals will not grow cold as long as they have cedar to smoke. I knew that. I knew to pray to the fire with cedar, to offer cedar, to talk, to implore, even beg with cedar. I sensed when I used the cedar that I impressed them; a 'Clay Kid' who could keep a fire going in the rain impressed them, but they didn't show it. I was not one of them. They couldn't allow me to be one of them, but I was okay at that moment because I loved fire. Just being with the fire, I was happy.

When the rocks were hot enough for the ceremony, I expected to be sent away, but to my surprise Kanojaohweh, Big Kettle, looked directly at me and said in a voice that surprised me with its strength:

"Hehnoke, Relative, so, come over here under the roof. Get a towel from the box. Get dry. Nephew will take care of the fire."

"Haksotko:wah, nyah weh, thank you." I used the very formal "my great-grandfather" in return.

"Huh!" he chuckled at my formality. Or maybe not; maybe he was chuckling at my pronunciation!

I wrapped a towel around my head and sat down.

Big Kettle looked at me. He may have been shriveled and creased with age lines, but he had power and I held him in awe.

"There's a story about balance my ancestors used to tell: 'A man went to his cornfield one day when the corn was knee-high and found it had been devoured by corn bugs. The man raked the cornhusks together and burned them. In doing that, he burned the corn bugs too.

"A spirit appeared. 'Why are you burning my relatives, the corn bugs?' the spirit said.

"'They ate my corn. How shall I feed my children?' the man said. 'Am I not worthy?'

"'Yes, you are worthy,' the spirit said. 'Go home. Come back in four days.'

"Four days later the man came back to his field. He found baskets, tightly woven, full of corn, beans, and squash – enough for all winter.

"The next year the man remembered what happened the year before. He went early and when the corn bugs came, he set them on fire and killed them all before they could eat his plants.

"Once again the spirit appeared, 'Why did you kill my relatives?'

"The man said, 'Your relatives wanted to eat my plants. What am I to eat? Am I not worthy?'

"'Go away and come back in four days'," said the spirit.

"Four days later the man came back and saw his corn stalks were as high as the antlers of a moose and the ears of corn were enormous. He tried to pick the first ear. It was not an ear; it was a hornet's nest. All the ears were hornets' nests. The man runs but the hornets bite him anyways."

Big Kettle paused to dry his forehead and eyes. He blew his nose into his towel, checked it, rubbed it together and then put the towel down beside him.

"In the old days we used controlled burns all the time to clear the fields, the thickets, blackberries, grasses, corn stalks. Then the Clay People outlawed our old ways of burning. Our crops were weakened. The corn bugs strengthened. That law didn't understand balance.

"The path of the Clay People is a straight line," Big Kettle went on, his eyes riveted on the fire. "Our way is a circle. A straight line cuts a circle and divides it, weakens it."

Big Kettle's words sank in. The story, "Clay People," upsetting the balance, not understanding the way of the land; in their minds I am like those who use fungicides. They showed me their ways, they even loved me, but the truth was, I upset the balance. I was Clay, forever Clay in their house; a straight line in their circle.

I turned away, fighting back tears. It was wrong to turn my back on my elders, but I didn't want them to see me cry. Indian boys don't cry. I held myself around my waist and tried to stop the heaving and the pain in my heart. That was not good. They would see me grieving more for myself than for Oskee, I'm sure. I had to face this.

"But why?" I wailed, whirling and facing them, tears still running on my face. "I don't want to be with Clay People. I'm ashamed of Clay People…"

Big Kettle regarded me with care and said, "There's a Clay People story about a man named Moses. He lives a good life; he's got no problems. One day he has a vision. He sees a bush; it's on fire. It burns and burns but the fire never eats the bush. So, it's the Fire Spirit. Somehow Moses knows that so he goes closer and the Bush, still on fire, speaks! 'I hear the people crying,' the Bush said."

Big Kettle took his gaze from the fire and put it on me. It felt to me as though in doing that he left elsewhere and re-entered here.

"For us the Stones are the Burning Bush. The Stones hear our cries."

He paused, pursing his lips, tilling his thoughts

"You are good with the Fire. You respect it, and for that it responds to you; it has already changed your life. We see that. But you don't understand the Fire Spirit. The Burning Bush, the Stone People, that's all from Good Mind. Trouble is, Good Mind has a Twin Brother. His name is 'Hanikoetke. It means, 'He Leaves Nothing For Others!' If Hanikoetke put fire in that Burning Bush, his fire would leave nothing but ashes."

Kanojaohweh looked back to the Fire and paused as if drawing strength. I looked at the lines and creases in his face and the wisps of thin white hair sneaking out from beneath a broad-brimmed straw hat and thought, oddly enough, that *if he is eighty years old he was born in 1872.* 1872, that was inconceivable to me. Who knows? He was probably older than that. He was probably born in the 1860's.

Big Kettle smiled and nodded a slight 'yes.'

"Jichohsahse has blessed you; she took your life into her hands. Your life *will* always *be* in her hands. She has a plan for you and it is not with us. It's near time for your 'coming of age.' Jichohsahse has told us that you must become a man of your *own* people."

Big Kettle's kind, glistening old eyes tunneled into me. He pronounced Jichosahse with that nasal sound and it took me a few seconds to recognize the word. I must have had a confused look on my face, so he continued:

"Have you seen a clown dance at a powwow?"

I nodded no. I'd never been to a powwow.

"He dances backwards, hops around on one leg, always on the edge of falling over, strutting, running into people, acting all drunk and stupid. But he never falls over. He never hurts anyone. He never loses control. It takes a very good dancer to be such a bad dancer."

I was half-listening. Why should I? They've decided. I'm not one of them.

"She wants you to learn how to dance on the straight line of your people. Get good at it so you can be bad at it. Then, one day, you can teach them to dance in a circle."

"Is it not enough that I can build a fire and keep it going in the rain?" I said somewhat bitterly while looking at Haksot.

He stopped ignoring me, finally looked at me, but there was no expression.

"It's enough…" Haksot said, his voice rasping, "…for now," and looked away.

He taught me so much; he asked me to climb the tree! Now, he can't even look at me? I felt downright betrayed. The lump in my throat was so big I couldn't speak. I dried my face and hair and tears with the towel, tossed it at the box of towels, turned to walk away, and was stopped in my tracks.

It was Singing Woman, just there, dressed in light, dressed in music, her song filling the voice inside my head, and I instantly I understood what the old men were teaching.

"Grandson," Haksot said abruptly, and just as quickly the light and the music and the song were quiet.

I turned back. "What?"

"Do you remember the story about Three Arrows? How he brought Fire to the People? How it was a gift from Good Mind?"

I nodded "yes."

"The Good Mind Fire is lit in your heart now. It will never consume you. Your Spirit friend; she'll make sure of that."

The way I was taught, we should never leave a ceremony without eating. It's disrespectful. Breaking bread together is an essential part of every one of their ceremonies. If we had left without eating, they would have assumed we were shunning them. Even so, I stayed grudgingly and pretty much at Father's insistence.

I'm glad we did. Once the old men came out of the Burning Water Lodge, the whole atmosphere of the ceremony changed. All of a sudden it was a celebration of life. Even Nick came down from his room. Gramma told him to wash the tear steaks from his face before he joined in.

What was most amazing was that Gramma asked my father to say the blessing over the food, which he did without invoking Jesus and by saying 'Haswenio' instead of God!

After that, not everybody, but a number of people came up and shook his hand and then smiled at me. Norma, Oskee's mother, put my head in her hands and looked hard at me. I was afraid she was going to blame me for Oskee's death, but instead she said, "It wasn't your fault." That felt so good I got tears in my eyes. I hadn't even brushed them away when Mavis kissed me on the forehead and called me "Hegeh." It means "little brother."

"Nick…" I suddenly said out loud as Dad and I passed the border of the rez on the drive home that night. "…he didn't want to talk to me. You think he was mad because Mavis was nice to me at the end? She's never so much as given me the time of day before…"

"Nick's not angry with you. He's hurting; he's in a lot of pain and his heart is closed off. Nick needs a lot of love and compassion right now. To the Seneca, time doesn't matter, everything is a place; a person is a place where a Soul resides. Right now the door to his Soul is closed."

I pondered that, my mind trying to use what he said to put that whole day into the perspective of a person being a place.

We drove in silence for several miles, during which I knew, I just *knew*, there was something on the tip of his tongue begging to be said.

"What?"

"What?" he answered.

"You want to tell me something."

Dad laughed. "Seems like Minnie has taught you how to read minds." Dad kept his eyes on the road while he talked. "You wondered why I let you spend so much time with the Indians even though it's going to cost me…? Reality isn't found in words; it's taught by experiences. I wanted you to have the experience of their knowledge. That's why."

I sat in the passenger seat of our Chevy and let my mind drift back over the last two years. We were turning off Main onto Grove Street before I came back to the moment and asked, "What do you mean, cost you?"

"Your mother is going to win custody of you. You'll be going to live with her… and your grandfather. Maybe it's for the best. You'll probably will go to private schools, your intellect will finally get challenged, and… I admit, I'm not much of a parent. But I have no regrets. The way you were taught by those elders… never obvious, never exacting, without attachment… and just so you know, they don't cut loose those who aren't ready."

"I don't want to be cut loose. I don't want to leave here!"

"I know, but the choice isn't yours. The court doesn't care what you want, what children want."

"The straight line …"

Dad looked at me. "You lost me there."

"Big Kettle told me I have to learn to dance on the straight line. The Judge's world; that's what the straight line is." Then I remembered, "Of course! Months ago Gramma told me Mother was coming for me. She knew all along…"

He looked at me and smiled. "You know she hears voices from the future, don't you? She's probably known things about you since the day she met you."

He pulled the Chevy into the driveway, turned off the motor, but didn't open his door. Instead, we sat in the dark for a moment. I realized there was something else he wanted to say.

Finally he asked, "Before we left tonight, Minnie said to me, 'Tell him my name. It will help him understand.' Has Minnie ever told you her Seneca name?"

I thought for a while and then, "No, she never told me, but Nick did, once. It's a really long word that means 'Firefly' in English."

Father shook his head. "That's her childhood name; her name up until she was seventeen."

"When Mavis was born?" I asked, though it was almost a statement.

"Yes, after a Seneca woman gives birth the first time her name changes. Her Long House name became 'Neoko:tajee'."

I shook my head, "Neoko is deer, what's 'tajee'?"

"When it's used as a suffix, it means black…"

"Black Deer?"

"The irony is amazing," Father chuckled. "Think tail."

"Black... Tail? Her name is 'Blacktail Deer?' But that means... she said never to follow..."

"Never to follow – yes, she got that name because in those days she was very beautiful and very... captivating. But that's not her only name. As a respected wolf clan mother, she also has a Spirit Name. I never knew what that was until tonight – when she asked me to tell you. I don't know the Seneca word or words, but it translates in English as the Northern Lights, only she said you would know her as Singing Woman."

<<< >>> :: <<< >>>
<<< >>> :: <<< >>>

# ABOUT THE AUTHOR
## <<< :: >>>

Raised in a border town of the Cattauraugus Seneca Indian Reservation where his father was chaplain at the Indian school, **Glenn Schiffman** has lived around or with American Indians all of his life and counts many relatives among American Indians. He has Vision-Fasted 12 times, sat in on numerous traditional healing ceremonies, has been a fire keeper at 15 Sun Dances and danced in 8 others. Since 2010 he's been a Pipe-Keeper of a traditional Sun Dance on the Pine Ridge Reservation in South Dakota.

Glenn has built more than 100 sweat lodges in all regions of the US and has personally conducted over 1000 Inipi (sweat lodge) ceremonies. He has been interviewed by print and TV news organizations including CNN, and appeared in TV docu-dramas about Native American lore. In addition, he served as the Go-Between on a documentary about a dance by Arapaho to celebrate the 1994 release of wolves into Yellowstone National Park.

In 1990, Glenn produced a CD and laser disc educational program for IBM's Eduquest Group based on the book "Black Elk Speaks" and was a writer on the Eduquest publication of The Declaration of Independence. He has also written historical essays and literary reviews for Salem Press, the McGill Annual Literary Review, and the Newbury Library.

In addition to his novels, Glenn has created a DVD demonstrating "The Thanksgiving Prayer of the Iroquois Peoples." He's currently writing a book about "Places of Emergence" and collaborating on a blog and video series exploring: "What does it mean to be a Human Being."

Glenn is a co-founder of **Western Gate Roots & Wings Foundation**, a non-profit which counsels youth, uninitiated adult men and returning veterans in collaboration with Native Elders and counselors at Home Boys Industries (Los Angeles). His academic degrees include a BA in History (Knox College), an MFA in Creative Writing (San Francisco State University), and a Masters in Spiritual Counseling (University of Santa Monica).

*Glenn's blog:*  http://RootsandWingsFoundation.blogspot.com

*Roots & Wings Foundation*: www.WGRW.org

CPSIA information can be obtained at www.ICGtesting.com
Printed in the USA
LVOW04s0103061015

457040LV00012B/54/P

9 781499 183351